the
WELL-KEPT
Secret

A WISHVILLE MYSTERY

kari lee townsend
NATIONAL BESTSELLING AUTHOR

OLIVERHEBERBOOKS

To all those who dare to dream and have the courage to follow their hearts wherever that might take them. May your lives be filled with excitement and adventure!

A very special thank you to my fabulous publisher, Tanya Anne Crosby —who's so supportive and one amazingly talented author—for giving me the courage to step out of my comfort zone and try something new. This one's for you 😊

Once Upon a Time...

LONG BEFORE WISHVILLE was ever a name on a map, Vermont was wild and unclaimed. In the early 1700s it was a land of uncolonized frontier, mountains cloaked in whispering forests, its valleys hidden from the world. Beneath that wilderness, however, there was already life—immortal beings called Dwellers, who had existed since the time of dinosaurs. Their magical wishing well was their portal to the world above, and for centuries they roamed the land freely, unseen, moving like silver shadows through the earth.

But after 1730, the land began to change. Land grants were issued, settlers came with their axes and their prayers, and Vermont shifted from wilderness to frontier. In time, a band of English settlers stumbled upon the wishing well and built their homes around it. They called their little settlement Wishville, soon realizing the well was no ordinary spring. Its waters shimmered with promise, granting endless wishes to those who dared whisper them into its depths. And in time, those whispers led them to discover the Dwellers, and the glowing realm of Elarion beneath the well.

At first, wonder reigned, but human wonder quickly soured

into human greed. The settlers wanted more than wishes—they wanted immortality. They sought to drink from Dweller rivers like a fountain of youth, and they began to mine the crystals and pluck the herbs that grew with magic. The Dwellers resisted, and war broke out between the two peoples. Many died on both sides. Though immortal, Dwellers were not invincible. Like heroes of legend, each had a weakness—a single hidden vulnerability, like Superman and his kryptonite. And when those weaknesses were discovered, Dwellers fell.

The war might have destroyed them all if not for the Council of Elders in Elarion. They proposed a treaty: humans would remain above in Wishville, and Dwellers would remain below in Elarion. The wishing well would be sealed, kept as the boundary between worlds. Wishville's town council agreed on one condition. That the Dwellers allow the people one festival for each season, where wishes could still be made. The Dwellers consented with a condition of their own. During each WishFest, tokens forged in Elarion would be given out, one per person, and the well itself would choose a single wish to grant.

Thus WishFest was born.

The treaty was signed over three hundred years ago by Wishville's founders and the Elders of Elarion. From that day on, the Guardian of the Well was tasked with upholding it. The rules were clear: one wish granted each season. If ever a festival ended without a wish being chosen, the treaty would be broken and war might resume.

The well itself was no Dweller and no god, but an entity all its own. Its power was only to grant wishes, and even that power was limited by the Elders, who acted as a lamp contains a genie. To the people of Wishville, though, the well was miracle enough. Over the generations, as those first settlers died, the truth blurred into folklore. Elarion became a whispered legend, the Dwellers faded into fairy tales, and the well became a curiosity with no mention of the portal—some believed, some scoffed, and most called it nothing more than myth. A lost city, perhaps, like Atlantis beneath the sea.

Today, a handful of people are still searching for the truth...

CHAPTER
One

THEY SAY WISHVILLE, Vermont was carved by the fingers of fate—etched into a fold of the Green Mountains where the forests breathe secrets and the lakes mirror the sky. A postcard town wrapped in pine and birch, it shimmered with a quiet magic most people couldn't name, let alone see.

From the surface, it was charming.

Quaint shops lined Main Street—painted in pastel hues with flower boxes spilling petunias in summer and icicles in winter. The café's bell jingled like clockwork with every gossip-laced coffee order. The mountains embraced the town like protective arms, and Lake Mistfall lay nestled to the north, perpetually veiled in morning mist so thick it looked enchanted.

And what might give them that idea?

Maybe because it was.

The wishing well stood on the edge of a clearing in the forest up a short hill at the end of town—made of ancient stone, its rim mossy and smooth from a thousand hopeful hands. To everyone else, it was just a relic from an old folktale. A good luck charm. A backdrop for selfies.

To me, it was a doorway.

Once upon a time, Dwellers existed in the mountains of

Vermont, roaming free since the time of dinosaurs, living beneath the earth with the well as their portal to the world above. When settlers moved into the area and discovered the magical well that granted wishes, it led them to Elarion and the Dwellers below. The humans invaded their world, searching for the fountain of youth in its rivers and mining its crystals. War broke out and many people died on both sides. Dwellers are immortal, but each one has a unique weakness they can die from if discovered.

Elarion's Council of Elders proposed a peace treaty that Dwellers would remain below the well and humans would remain above ground with the portal being sealed. Wishville's town council agreed on one condition. A festival would be held once per season with one lucky person's wish granted. The well would choose the wishes and grant them, but the Elders would be allowed to control the well. The Elders agreed to the terms but added one last condition of their own. Coins thrown into the well at any other time won't work. Only magical wish tokens provided by the Guardian of the Well during the festival will work.

With that, WishFest was born.

Over time, the enchanted city of Elarion, ethereal creatures called Dwellers, and the magical wishing well became legend and eventually faded into folklore, with no mention of a portal or where the city was located. Today the tradition remains that four times a year, citizens of Wishville and visitors alike gather around the well to toss in a special token and make a wish. Legend has it that one lucky person each season will have their wish come true at the end of the festival. The locals treated it like a novelty—toss in a token at any time during the festival, make a wish, and laugh it off with a selfie. If wishes do come true, most chalk it up to wishful thinking, but some speculate the legend is real and continue looking for the lost city.

No one knew for sure the real reason WishFest came about and the importance of the well... Not for centuries. That was my job. To remember its history, keep the festivals going, and protect its legacy.

And I'd been doing exactly that for the last century.

No matter the season, the weather in Wishville could be unpredictable—sunshine one minute and mist, rain or even snow the next. My job involved being outdoors and in the woods, so layering my clothing was key. Today I wore spandex-blended hiking pants, waterproof socks and boots, and a dry wicking short sleeve t-shirt.

I adjusted my fawn brown canvas crossbody bag over my sage green lightweight waterproof jacket and made my way through town to the path up the hill to the forest clearing in silence. A breeze rustled the tulip beds that framed the square. Spring was still new here—birds just beginning to return, trees stretching tender green fingers toward the sun. Everything looked fresh and alive.

Everything except me.

You're brooding again, Lyra, Vex said, winding between my ankles. His voice was velvet in my mind—Mind Whispering was one of his many tricks, though he only used it when he wanted to be annoying. Which was often.

"Not brooding," I murmured, glancing down at my special cat. "Just watching."

Same thing. You get that squinty, poetic look when you're brooding. Very tragic forest nymph instead of modern WishFest Chair.

I glanced down at him. "You're not exactly inconspicuous with that glowing pendant around your neck, making you look less like your cat half and more like your Whispen side."

Vex's black fur glistened faintly, like the surface of the well under starlight. His tail flicked proudly. *I'm accessorized. There's a difference.* His tiny well-shaped pendant around his neck swayed as we reached the clearing, and he padded toward the stone well then leaped onto its rim.

I laughed out loud and followed him, then rested a hand on the ancient stones. They were warm, pulsing faintly beneath my fingers. The magic was restless, and so was I. As Guardian of the

Well, it was my job to ensure the centuries-old treaty between humans and Dwellers remained intact.

This had been my mother's job...before she vanished.

Three-hundred-years ago, at the time the treaty was signed, my mother met my father, Josiah Wells, who was Wishville's Chronicler and poet. Against all odds, they fell in love and had me—the one and only half-blood. My father was a mortal human, and my mother was an immortal Dweller. Full Dwellers had hair and eyes like liquid gemstones.

Me? I was something in between.

I didn't age. Actually, I did, but slowly. One human year was equivalent to ten Dweller years, so I looked nearly thirty but was really almost three-hundred-years old and took over as Guardian of the Well a century ago when my mother went missing. I tucked my long, thick hair behind my ear and the early morning sunlight reflected off the streaks of burgundy, green, gold, and dark brown curls—like layers of the forest floor in autumn.

Looking over the edge of the well at the water, my amber gold eyes reflected back at me. They weren't quite human, not quite Dweller, but just enough of both to be neither. People often asked if I had highlights or if I wore colored contacts, having no idea everything on me was all natural...and centuries old.

I pressed a palm to the spiral pendant at my throat. It was silver, ancient, both a key and a curse.

Just then, a sound like distant bells clattered down the path. I turned to see three figures approaching—each as out of place as a carnival at a coronation—and I couldn't help but smile.

Tilda "Tilly" Nettleblossom led the charge, her patchwork skirt rustling with every step and her gray braid wrapped in a vine of what might've been actual lavender. A retired herbalist, she now ran a thrifted spell jar booth called *Bibbidi, Bottles & Boo* in the marketplace. She was sassy and sharp-tongued, and she kept a journal of ominous dreams she swore predicted the town's disasters.

"The well's humming funny again." She peered past me to the stones. "I felt it in my spleen."

Behind her jingled Maribelle "Belle" Crimp, dripping in sequins and sporting a feathered shawl like she was late for the opera. The dramatic, theatrical, gossip connoisseur was a former opera singer turned town crier who wore way too much sparkle and jingled when she walked. These days she trained pigeons to carry secret notes for security purposes, instead of using a cell phone, but they mostly just delivered them to the bakery and she had no idea why, suspecting some sort of interference.

"You won't believe what happened last night." She shivered. "A pigeon dropped a ribbon in my tea. That means a secret's about to unravel."

Dottie "Dot" Quench brought up the rear, her polka dot clothes matching her polka dot mug. "Trust the clumsy pigeon's omen and hold onto your undergarments. You do shop at *Silken Secrets*, after all." Owner of *The Quench & Snoop Tea House*, she sold wildly inaccurate fortunes in tea leaves. She was sweet but totally loopy, believing she was part mermaid from her father's side.

"I sense a cold spot. Definitely a spectral shift." She blinked, her eyes looking owllike behind her oversized round spectacles that put Elton John's to shame. "Or maybe *my* undergarments have started unraveling."

Tilly stood there shaking her head and looking appalled.

"The Wellies," I murmured to Vex.

A trio of nosy, meddling, lovable older women who were best friends. They believed they were the unofficial guardians of the wishing well, and possibly the whole town, becoming my shadow with unsolicited advice more often than not. They were part folk-lore-keepers, part busybodies, and they insisted they knew *more than the mayor* when it came to town secrets.

Of course, none of them had real magic, but their intuition was suspiciously spot-on at times. Some believed they were secretly Dwellers from the legend living among us, while others just thought they were old and weird. I knew they were harmless.

Yet they were always around when trouble stirred.

"The *watchers* have arrived...again," Vex muttered, hopping down from the rim with a tail swish of disdain.

The three older women flanked the well like sentries, their hands on hips and eyes narrowed.

"You feel it too, don't you, Lyra?" Tilly asked. "The magic? I just know it's real."

I offered a diplomatic smile. "The idea that the well might be magical is the appeal of WishFest for many, but the well remains a mystery."

"The feeling seems stronger than usual this time." Dot Tilted her head. "My tea leaves formed the shape of a badger this morning. You know what that means."

"No," I said. "Not even a little."

"Reckoning," she answered ominously.

I bit back another smile. I'd known these women since they were born and had to erase their memory of me many times as they'd grown to retirement age. They now felt like three great aunties to me, and the closest thing to family I'd had in a long time. I dreaded the thought of having to erase them again in the future.

Belle tossed a glitter scarf over her shoulder and gave me a knowing smirk. "You've got the look of someone caught between two storms, child. Don't try to play coy with me. What's troubling you?"

I opened my mouth but had no idea what to say to that.

"You girls let Lyra do her thing," Tilly finally declared. "She knows more than she lets on. We'll be close if she needs us. Holler if the well starts spitting frogs."

With that, the trio turned and floated—more like waddled—down the path, leaving a faint trail of glitter, lavender, and dried sardines in their wake.

Vex groaned. *They get weirder every year.*

"And that's what I love about them, but they're not wrong," I said softly, touching the well again. "Something's brewing."

He sighed. *Then let's hope your fan club doesn't make things worse.* "Ms. Wells?"

I sucked in a sharp breath, startled, and then frowned. Normally, nothing or no one could sneak up on me. The voice was deep. Smooth like a stone skipping across water, but heavy with authority. I turned...and blinked.

He was taller—maybe six-foot-four inches—and more muscular than I remembered from the picture in his file. I had a file on everyone in town. Broad-shouldered, dark buzzed hair, trim beard, and intense storm-grey eyes that didn't miss much. Dark Gray sport coat, light gray button down shirt, black tie, blue jeans, and black leather boots. He wore his badge like it was fused to his belt, as if a part of him had been carved out and replaced with duty.

Chief Holden Thorn.

I shook off my odd reaction to him and pasted on a friendly smile as I held out my hand. "Chief Thorn I presume? So nice to finally meet you. You're up early."

He gave my hand a firm shake, then drew his shaggy eyebrows together for a moment as if he'd felt the connection between us too and quickly let go. Looking away, he surveyed the forest clearing as if it were a back alley in a big city. "I wanted to see the festival preparations for myself."

"Then you're just in time for the start of the chaos. It takes a bit of time to pull each festival together." I gestured toward the line of vendors setting up their booths beneath tents—homemade candles, lavender soaps, charm bracelets, wish jars, and more. The main stores were down the short hill in town around the square with the festival grounds up top by the well. "This is Wishville at its most festive. Everything comes alive during the festival." I beamed proudly.

He didn't smile. Just arched a thick brow. "I read the town ordinances. These festivals happen every season?"

"Yes." I straightened. "We might be part of the twenty-first century, but our town is steeped in tradition. We hold a new festival for each solstice and equinox. It keeps the town spirit alive."

"Or invites trouble." His gaze scanned the open, vulnerable grounds with military precision. "You know how many outsiders show up for these things? How many variables that introduces?"

"Joyful ones?" I offered.

He gave me a look that could've wilted flowers. "I'm not here to play referee for glitter and wishes, Ms. Wells."

"Of course you're not. That's *Sheriff* Trip's job."

Holden narrowed his eyes. "My job is to protect this town."

I stepped forward, refusing to cower from his verbal thorns. "So is mine."

He grunted. "Is it?"

He suddenly wasn't nearly as intriguing as I'd thought. I counted to ten before responding. "I represent the Historical Society. WishFest is my responsibility as Chair. It's part of our heritage." I nodded, settling my hands on my hips.

He studied me in silence, as if trying to figure out what I *wasn't* saying.

I didn't flinch, but I could feel Vex's energy tighten like a coiled spring.

"This town doesn't need four festivals a year," Holden said finally. "One, maybe two. We could space them out. Reduce the risks."

My stomach knotted. "That's not an option."

"Why?"

I hesitated. The real answer—that the treaty required seasonal wishes to be granted to maintain the balance between worlds, that a skipped festival could break centuries of peace—would get me laughed out of town.

Or worse...locked in his jail.

"Because the festivals mean everything to this town," I said instead. "People build their entire year around these traditions and the income they bring to Wishville. Reducing them would cause disruption."

"Then we manage the disruption." He shrugged. "You can't cling to *tradition* just because it's comfortable. Too many outsiders bring danger."

"I'm not." My voice came out sharper than I intended. "I'm doing what's necessary, and from *my* experience, outsiders bring revenue."

He looked at me for a long time as if he were trying to figure me out. "I don't believe in wishes," he said quietly. "They don't actually come true no matter how much you want them to."

A silence fell between us.

I saw it then—the edge of grief in his eyes, and I remembered his file. He'd lost his father recently, and his mother long before that. The file said childbirth for her. The press said collateral damage for him.

Holden was a former marine turned homicide detective. A criminal he had put away had escaped and targeted the only family he had left. So, Holden had changed course and applied for the Chief of Police position, moving from big city Boston to small town Wishville to outrun his ghosts.

But this town had a way of conjuring them instead.

"I'm sorry," I said, softer now. "About your father."

He looked surprised. Vulnerable for a second.

I winced. That was information I shouldn't know. "I was good friends with the former chief's wife before they retired to Florida," I said by way of explanation.

His wall snapped back into place, and he nodded once, sharply. "Thank you."

Vex jumped from the well and brushed past his leg.

Holden stiffened, his eyebrows narrowing. "Your cat's eyes just changed color."

"Vex is...unique."

Holden eyed him warily. "Is he part of the festival too?"

Vex rolled his eyes and padded off.

I smirked. "He's more management than entertainment."

Holden gave me a reluctant nod. "Keep me updated. If

anything seems off—even the small things—I want to know. And don't think this is the end of our discussion about festival frequency."

"Of course." We could *discuss* all he wanted, but I would never agree to it.

He turned and walked away, his silhouette sharp against the rising sun, his presence lingering like smoke in the air.

Vex returned to my side, his ears twitching. *He's trouble.*

"Maybe." He might be cynical and grumpy, but there was something about him that had drawn me in from the moment I'd heard his voice and seen his face. A connection I couldn't deny, but I had no clue what it meant or what to do about it.

I don't trust him, Vex said with a purr.

"You don't trust anyone." I looked up at the sky—crisp, blue, unmarred by clouds—and down at the well. The festival would start soon, the spring wishes would roll in, and something else would descend upon Wishville. I could feel it. I didn't know what yet, but the well did.

And the well never lied.

CHAPTER
Two

I WAITED until the town exhaled its last breath for the night: when the streetlamps turned on, cars returned home, houses were locked, and silence settled over Wishville like a heavy quilt. I made my way to the forest, moonlight glinting off the rim of the wishing well, the stone glistening with dew. The shadows of sycamores stretched long and skeletal across the cobblestones, and the only sound was the faint trickle of water echoing up from the depths.

The well called to me. It always had.

I brushed my fingers across the ancient runes carved into the inner rim, warm and familiar. I whispered the incantation under my breath, and the spiral pendant around my neck glowed silver in response, spinning slowly, matching the hum that thrummed up from deep below as the grate that sealed the well vanished.

Beside me, Vex leaped onto the edge and blinked his ever-changing eyes. *Do you want me to come?* he asked through our bond.

"No," I whispered. "I need him to listen. He won't if you're making faces behind him the whole time."

I don't make faces.

I gave him a look.

Fine. I enhance *the conversation, he amended with a tail twitch, but if he raises his voice, I'm coming through, Chief Enforcer or not.*

I slipped one leg over the side and then the other. "I'll be back before sunrise." Then I pushed myself off the edge and let go.

Falling into the well wasn't like falling at all.

It was more like slipping through a seam in the world. The air turned thick, cool, and strangely alive around me. The stone walls faded, replaced by light—streams of silver and soft blue, like being caught in the currents of a slow-moving dream. When I landed, it was in silence, into a realm that was timeless.

Elarion stretched before me, radiant and haunting.

Bioluminescent flowers bloomed along the hillsides, glowing like constellations against the crystal pathways. The sky—if you could call it that—shimmered with soft golden orbs floating in gentle orbits, casting a dreamlike light over everything. Waterfalls of liquid light cascaded from cliffs above into pools that rippled with iridescent colors of memories rather than reflections, their sounds like whispered lullabies in a forgotten language.

The air was always thick here, not oppressive but heavy with magic. My hair drifted around me in slow motion, as if I were under water. The streaks of burgundy, gold, green, and brown flowed around my shoulders in silent waves, the colors more vivid here beneath the veil than above in Wishville.

My skin was pale and smooth like my mother's, but I had a birthmark on the back of my neck like my father, which was why I always wore my hair down in Elarion. A Dweller's skin was flawless and unmarked.

One of my powers was the use of a Moonveil, which manipulated moonlight for illusions, cloaking, or calming emotions. That was why I transported at night so I wouldn't be seen. Before I left my home in Wishville, I'd changed out of my earthly hiking clothes into my Elarion ceremonial robes—garments that mirrored the quiet magic of the natural world. The fabric was woven from threads the color of moss and river stone, laced with accents of muted copper and soft, leaf green.

Unlike the fluid shimmer of Dweller silks, mine had a gentle, grounded texture, like bark after rainfall—sturdy, alive, and deeply rooted.

A sash of dusky rose as soft as a mountain breeze cinched my waist—a nod to the wildflowers that grew near the wellspring that meant so much to my parents. The sleeves flared at the wrists, revealing an underlay of pale sky-blue fabric that rippled faintly when I moved, whispering of wind and open fields.

I bore no inherited seal—neither my father's human lineage nor my mother's Dweller crest claimed me fully. Instead, I wore a seal of my own making—a woven emblem stitched over my heart with shaking hands and stubborn resolve. A sapling growing from a cracked stone, its roots entwining with a water current that looped into the shape of an eye. The leaves shimmered with silver thread—Dweller light—and the stone glinted with flecks of brown and green—earth-born resilience.

Symbolic of survival and harmony, not status.

My mother's crest colors had once been glacier blue and pearl white, and her seal was a crescent moon cradling a drop of rain. Beautiful, elegant, but distant. Mine was different. Mine was alive.

I felt him before I saw him. The atmosphere changed, the current shifted, and my heart skipped a beat like it always did when I was near him.

Chief Calderis.

He emerged from the far side of the bridge that crossed the Lirien River, where the water sparkled like stardust and the stones glowed faintly beneath his steps. He moved like liquid: elegant, tall—six-foot-ten inches—and dangerous in the quiet way a blade is dangerous when resting in its sheath.

His eyes, the color of rushing water, churned with fluid motion even in stillness. His hair streamed behind him in slow, shimmering waves, a cascade of silver that caught the ambient light like moonlit silk. His robes were dark, trimmed in cobalt and adorned with symbols of his station—Chief of the Enforcers. The seal, a twisting crest resembling flowing water around a sunstone, rested on his chest. His body was long and lean, like a swimmer's build but wrapped in power.

Walking beside him was his best friend from childhood and fellow enforcer, Drelian, a slightly shorter and more aquamarine version of him.

I straightened to my full five-foot-ten-inch height—short in this world—as he approached, careful not to show how the sight of him always made me feel a little too mortal. A little too small.

Not quite good enough in his eyes, even though he'd never said so.

He said something to Drelian, who glanced my way and nodded once, then headed in the opposite direction.

"Lyra Wells." Calderis stopped just short of me. His voice echoed slightly, low and clear, his displeasure of my double name evident. Dwellers only had first names and titles, but I refused to give up my human father's last name. "I expected you would come."

"You always say that." I brushed a curl out of my face. "And yet you always look annoyed when I do."

"That's because you only come when there's trouble involved." He studied me carefully. "I don't like trouble."

I resisted the urge to roll my eyes and stepped onto the bridge. It arched gracefully over the Lirien river, the crystalline structure warm beneath my slippers, thrumming faintly in response to our presence. Beneath us, silver fish darted through the illuminated water in synchronized patterns.

"I need your advi—er, counsel." I forced my voice to steady. Things were more formal in Elarion, even the language. "There's a problem above."

He raised a perfectly sculpted eyebrow, his eyes still rippling. "The treaty?"

"Not directly," I said, "but a new variable. A new Chief of Police, Holden Thorn."

His name made Calderis still. Just a tightening of his jaw and a narrowing of his eyes, but it was enough to reveal his wariness.

He didn't like unknowns. I was one, and now Holden was another. Calderis had always hated that he couldn't quite figure me out. I irritated him...

But I could tell, from the way his eyes lingered on my face a little longer than was necessary, that I intrigued him as well.

"He wants to reduce the frequency of WishFest," I explained, pulling my thoughts away from his hypnotic gaze. "He says the festival is too chaotic. That it brings too many outsiders and too much unpredictability."

Calderis folded his arms across his sculpted chest. "Then erase him."

"It's not that simple."

"It's *always* that simple."

"He's the chief. Erasing him will simply make him forget he ever met me. He's still going to hear about WishFest and want to alter the frequency, so what's the point?"

Calderis studied me with knowing eyes, his gaze probing. "You're not being objective."

"I *am*," I snapped, then paused. "But I'm also being careful."

"You're being emotional," he said cooly. "It's a dangerous indulgence."

"He's not the problem," I argued. "He just doesn't understand. He thinks he's protecting people."

"That's what humans always think before they destroy what they fear."

I walked a few paces down the bridge, letting the silence stretch. "He's lost people," I said at last. "His mother during his birth, and then later his father was murdered by someone he put away. He blames himself."

Calderis remained silent.

I turned to him. "You've lost people too." I paused for a moment. "Don't pretend you don't know what that does to someone." Being immortal simply meant you wouldn't die of natural causes. Being murdered was a whole different ball game. Even

Dwellers were vulnerable if someone discovered their weakness. The war had proven that.

"Loss sharpens," he replied, "or it poisons. Your chief sounds like someone still drinking from the cup."

"He's not *my* chief." My words came out harsher than I meant. "He's an obstacle...but not an enemy."

"You can't straddle the line forever, Lyra." Calderis held me captive with his gaze.

"I *am* part Dweller," I managed to get out.

"*And* part human," he countered without missing a beat. "Flawed. Mortal. Ill-suited to carry a role this sacred."

I flinched. "Yet here I am still doing it."

"Because I couldn't sway the council otherwise. They will always listen to the well." He looked away then reached into the folds of his robe and pulled out a clear crystal orb, small and faintly glowing—a Dweller's version of a cell phone but messages were sent by conjuring videos similar to using a crystal ball. I had one in Wishville so I could stay in touch. "My father asked for a report," he said. "The council watches more closely than you realize."

"Then tell them this." I took a moment to choose my words carefully. "The chief is not a threat. But if I erase his memory of me, it won't matter. He's the new police chief. He's still going to want to stop WishFest every season each time he meets me. I need him as an ally. He's the one person in Wishville capable of maintaining order when things inevitably go wrong."

He hesitated. "So, what do you propose?"

"I show him." I nodded, warming to the idea.

Calderis was already shaking his head. "We can't risk any human finding out the truth about our world."

"I'll show him something. A glimpse. A spark of truth. Just enough to stir up belief. Something to shift his perspective so he'll be on our side. I'm sure I can convince him how important these festivals are to keep Wishville thriving."

Calderis frowned. "And if that fails?"

"Then I'll let you erase him, and I'll find a way to get him transferred. But that may not stop the next chief from wanting to do the same thing."

He studied me again, his voice softer. "You walk a dangerous path, Lyra. My father believes your presence is a compromise. The Council tolerates you because they must. You are your mother's only child, and since she's gone, her title has fallen to you. That doesn't mean they trust you."

"Do *you* trust me?" I hated how much his answer mattered to me.

He didn't look away. "I trust the well, and it chose you. That's enough for me...for now." It was the closest thing to approval he'd ever given me.

I nodded, touching the spiral at my neck to feel closer to my mother. "I'll keep you informed."

"You'd better." His gaze met mine. "Because if your chief brings harm to the treaty, it won't be you who deals with him. It will be me. Trust me when I say I'll do more than erase him." With that, he turned and disappeared into the haze of the upper paths, his hair trailing like flowing water, leaving the scent of morning dew behind him.

I took a long breath, turned toward the well portal, and began the slow ascent home.

Back to the surface, back to Holden Thorn, and back to the space between two worlds.

None of which I fully belonged to.

CHAPTER
Three

THE MORNING RAYS of sunshine filtered through the wavy panes of leaded glass, painting ripples of yellow across the floorboards of my father's ancient house. It had been in his family since it was built. His family members had long since passed away, leaving me as the only heir. The house had remained a historical landmark until I became the Guardian of the Well a century ago when my mother went missing. I'd had to leave Elarion to live in Wishville, pretending to be fully human. I'd said yes to my role to be closer to her memory and had chosen to keep my father's house because it was all I had left of him.

The people in Wishville simply thought I was a long-lost relative come to claim my inheritance. And every time I out-aged them, I had to erase their memories and start over as if I were new in town all over again. It made for a lonely existence. I'd seen too many friends and boyfriends die along the way, so I finally put up a wall to protect my heart. I was still friendly with everyone.

I just didn't allow myself to get too close.

Dust floated through the beams like tiny spirits rising from the past. I moved slowly through the kitchen, the hem of my silk pajama pants whispering across the pine floor. The floor was worn smooth from centuries of footsteps—my ancestors, my father's, and now mine.

I really needed to renovate again.

It had been a human lifetime since I'd last done so, but I hadn't touched the floors since my father passed. I liked knowing I was still walking in his footsteps. I just kept patching whatever rotted, but maybe it was time I finally created a space of my own.

Not that I ever had anyone over to see it.

The kettle hissed on the iron stove. I inhaled the familiar scent of cedar, and the lingering ghost of pipe tobacco embedded deep in the walls. This house had outlived fires, floods, and generations of gossip. It sat stubbornly on the edge of the forest, half-swallowed by ivy, and only visible to those who knew where to look.

This place definitely needs a makeover, Vex said, reading my thoughts as he stretched across the back of an armchair, his tail flicking like a metronome. *Maybe a magical portrait or a floating banister. Something different and fun for a change. Aren't you bored?*

I poured hot water over loose chamomile and thyme. "I miss Elarion at times, too, but I'm glad to have you by my side. You're the only one who gets what it's like to be me. Maybe it's time to modernize things up a bit."

The silver spiral at my neck glinted in the morning sun as I moved through the living room, brushing my fingers across the bookshelves carved by my father's hands. This place had been his sanctuary, his dream rebuilt with sweat and stubborn love. The Dwellers hadn't cared for it. The humans had forgotten it.

But I cherished it.

Vex leaped gracefully onto the kitchen table and peered at the notepad I'd laid out. My mission for the day. Across the top, I'd written in pen:

SAVE OUR SEASONS: A Petition to Preserve WishFest.

I smoothed the page with my palm. "We'll get the signatures. We have to."

Vex sniffed. *If it comes down to you charming the townspeople or me biting the chief's ankle, I'm ready.*

"Let's hope it doesn't come to that."

Since everyone in town had heard of the legend, and no one knew that our wishing well was actually a portal, I would do anything to keep it that way. Let the people think we were capitalizing on the folklore. It was the few who believed Elarion was actually a lost city like Atlantis—possibly buried somewhere beneath the earth from some natural disaster long ago—I had to worry about.

Outside, the forest yawned open as we followed the winding trail toward town.

Spring had begun to wake the world—buds swelled on the branches of birch and sugar maple trees, robins called overhead, and the scent of thawing earth mixed with woodsmoke and pine needles. Magic floated faintly in the air, just beneath the surface— subtle, like the last note of a song you only half remember.

Wishville came into view, nestled between the hills like a secret.

Main Street had already begun to stir. Business signs were flipped to open, with window boxes below spilling early crocuses and trailing ivy. Sidewalks were swept clean, chairs in the barber shop were filling up, and old men played checkers on the sidewalk out front.

We headed first to *The Twisted Loaf*, its yellow door propped open and the smell of warm cinnamon clinging to the air like temptation.

"Lyra Wells!" Betsy Plum called, holding a tray of golden-brown cardamom knots. Her cheeks were dusted with flour, her hair pinned up with at least three long wooden spoons, and her apron proudly bore the words: *Flour Power*.

"Morning, Betsy," I said. "Smells divine, as always."

"Fresh from the oven." She beamed. "And don't think I didn't set one aside for you."

"Thank you." I winked at her.

Vex purred and stretched, his tail flicking against the bakery door, thinking, *None for the star of the show? How rude.*

I shot him a warning glance. No one could hear him except me, and I intended to keep it that way.

"He's such a character. If I didn't know better, I would swear his meows sound like words."

Before I could reply, a tinkling jingle and a cloud of lavender oil marked the arrival of the Wellies.

"Ah-ha!" Tilly waved her own mug of tea like a wand. "I told you she'd be here. My spleen never lies."

Belle twirled inside behind her in a blaze of sequins and a scarf full of bells. "I heard a pigeon whisper your name. You must need something important."

Dot clomped in last, wearing two different polka dot shoes. "Or you're here to deliver a prophecy. Either way, we approve."

"I'm collecting signatures to preserve WishFest," I said, bracing myself. "The chief wants to scale it back."

They gasped in unison as if I'd announced the sun was retiring.

"No!" Belle wailed. "What kind of monster trims the solstice from our seasons?"

Tilly already had a glitter pen out. "Write this down, Lyra. I predicted this. It was the tea leaves on the equinox. They formed the shape of a donkey holding a pad of paper."

Dot peered at the petition and sniffed. "That notepad was this petition. I knew it."

Despite their theatrics, all three signed with flair.

Not to be left out, Betsy grabbed a pen from her apron and signed with a flourish, topping the "y" in her name with a tiny loaf of bread. "You tell that handsome sourpuss, if he wants to cancel traditions, he'll have to take it up with the goddess of gluten."

"Consider him warned." I took the notepad from them with a nod.

As we stepped back out into the square, I could still hear Belle proclaiming to Betsy, "She has the aura of someone on the brink of a magical uprising. Probably indigestion."

Vex and I made our way down Main Street, where spring banners flapped from lampposts and the smell of lilac was in the air.

Next up was *Once Upon a Time*, the town's beloved—and rumored to be slightly haunted—bookstore. As we stepped inside, a cascade of windchimes jangled above us—not standard door chimes, but an actual tangle of silver spoons, feathers, antique keys, and dried herbs.

"Lyra!" Fiona Fitzwhistle's voice came from behind a stack of books labeled *Cursed Baking and What to do When You Find It*. She emerged in a swirl of plaid fabric, her orange curls caught up in a nest of bobby pins and feathers. Her glasses were tiny and slightly cracked.

"Are you putting mushrooms in the spring festival punch again?" I asked.

She looked mildly offended and raised her chin a notch. "They're *seasonal*, and they align the chakras...mostly."

Humans really thought they were the ones who had magical powers. I thought it was charming, but the other Dwellers often got irritated over the crazy shenanigans the Wishville residents partook in.

I handed her the petition. "We need signatures to keep Wish-Fest running as usual. The chief wants to limit it."

Fiona gasped like I'd told her we were banning fairy lights. "Next thing you know, he'll outlaw glitter." She signed in purple ink, adding a small constellation beneath her name. "He doesn't understand. WishFest isn't just about ribbons and booths, it's sacred. It keeps the town...*alive*."

I smiled and took the notepad back. "Exactly."

Next, Vex and I stopped by *The Dapper Den*, Gus Grimly's barber shop. He swore he'd cut Teddy Roosevelt's hair in a past life. He was a short, stocky, bald man with the most magnificent jet-black handlebar mustache, his pride and joy.

He signed while trimming a customer's sideburns, muttering,

"They always want to change things. Why can't they leave the good things alone?"

The men playing checkers out front agreed as they added their signatures.

Miss Ethel Frimble, a lonely grandmother who worked at the post office, signed three times—once for herself and once each for her elderly cats, Monsieur Buttons and Madame Frizzle.

"They're registered voters in spirit," she assured me.

By midday, my notepad was full of names, scrolls, and doodles. And all the while, the Wellies trailed me like magical bouncers—correcting rumors, waving feathers, and informing half the town that I was *probably* part water nymph.

"Just enough fae to be mysterious," Belle whispered to a tourist.

Tilly cackled. "Mark my words, the solstice winds have chosen her."

I sighed. "They're going to break the town before the treaty does."

Vex just smirked. *But they signed your petition, didn't they?*

"Yes," I said. "And started seventeen new rumors in the process."

I had another notepad tucked in my bag, but more than that, I had hope. Still, a knot twisted in my stomach.

"What if it's not enough?" I asked Vex as we sat near the fountain at the square, watching the wind ripple across the surface of the water.

They love you, he said simply. *And if today has taught us anything, it's that they love the festival, too. Look at all those signatures you got. Thorn can't defy the whole town. You can't give up.*

I nodded slowly, my fingers resting against the spiral pendant. "I just wish I didn't have to fight so hard to protect something they can't even see."

Vex nuzzled my boot, his voice gentler now. *That's why it matters. You see for them.*

I pushed the pressure from the Council of Elders and Calderis aside. I was making progress. I had a petition, a town full of eccentrics, and I planned to plead my case to the mayor. Our new grumpy police chief had no idea what he'd gotten himself into. May the gods help him...

Because WishFest wasn't going anywhere without a fight.

CHAPTER
Four

THAT AFTERNOON, I arrived at *Town Hall* and asked to see the mayor.

The chairs in the waiting room were the kind designed to make you squirm—thin cushions, stiff backs, and legs that wobbled just enough to imply disapproval. A bulletin board on the far wall proudly advertised last fall's leaf pile contest, a dog obedience seminar from two years ago, and an ad for guitar lessons taught by someone named "Shaky Jim."

All essential services, apparently.

I adjusted the notepad of signatures in my bag and took a steadying breath.

Relax, Vex said, perched on the windowsill like he owned the place. His eyes were pale blue this morning, almost translucent. *You've faced cursed mirrors, greedy Dwellers, and Fiona's mushroom punch. This is just a chief with a badge and a mayor with a gavel.*

"Which is somehow scarier," I muttered.

The door creaked open.

"Ms. Wells?" came the smooth voice of Assistant Mayor Doug Delaney, a thin man with a comb-over so precise it felt weaponized. "They're ready for you."

I followed him down the hall and into the room where town

decisions were made—painted a sensible cream with polished wood trim and a clock that ticked a little too loudly. Mayor Eliza Hemsworth sat at the head of the long table, her cardigan the same power red shade as her lipstick, her expression pleasant but unreadable.

And to her right sat Chief Holden Thorn, his arms crossed and eyes sharp.

"Ms. Wells," the mayor greeted me. "Thank you for coming. Please, have a seat."

I nodded and placed the notepad in front of them with care. "Thank you for seeing me. I come with a petition signed by a lot of residents, including small business owners, town elders, and concerned citizens."

Holden didn't reach for it. He just sat there and stared at me with that annoying arched brow.

Eliza adjusted her glasses and read the paper. "This is regarding the festival schedule, correct?"

"Yes, that is correct," I said. "WishFest isn't just tradition—it's our town's heartbeat. Scaling it back would disrupt our economy, our seasonal culture, and, frankly, the spirit of Wishville."

Holden finally spoke. "It also increases our risk of crime four times a year. Tourism spikes bring theft, petty crime, and over-stretched resources."

"Mayor Hemsworth." I locked eyes with her. "What we have here isn't just tradition for the sake of nostalgia. It's the rhythm our town is built on. Each festival is tied to the solstice or equinox—it honors nature, change, and belief. That means something to people. No other place has anything like this to bring visitors in. It makes us unique."

Holden gave a low scoff. "Being unique doesn't keep order."

"Being unique," I said evenly, "is what makes this town thrive. I do believe we hired *you* to keep order...unless you don't think you're capable of doing your job?"

That annoyingly high thick eyebrow finally came down. "You have no idea what I'm capable of, Ms. Wells." He stared me down.

"I guess we're about to find out since the people have spoken, Chief Thorn." I stared right back.

Eliza cleared her throat and skimmed through the signatures, nodding occasionally. "Betsy Plum...Fiona Fitzwhistle...Miss Ethel signed for herself and her cats again, I see."

"She's very passionate," I said.

The mayor set the notebook down and smiled faintly. "This is quite a turnout, but I admit, it's not enough for a majority vote. We *have* had more crime in recent years surrounding the festivals. Probably why we don't see Maisie Flint's name on the list. Her general store was broken into during the winter WishFest. If Chief Thorn thinks scaling the festivals back a bit is the answer, then maybe it's time we think of other streams of revenue."

"I'll get more people to sign," I blurted, desperate.

Holden leaned back in his chair and shook his head. "And if someone gets hurt this time? If the influx overwhelms our force? What then?"

Then you won't have crime, you frustrating man. You'll have all-out war, I wanted to shout. Instead, I met his gaze. "Then we work together to prevent it. You want tighter patrols? A volunteer marshal system? Fine. Let's coordinate. But canceling or condensing the festivals is not the answer. Doesn't it matter that the people have spoken? Don't you care about what they want?"

He didn't answer, but his jaw tightened.

I was starting to recognize his looks. He was calculating. Measuring. Not dismissing me, exactly...but he was far from being convinced.

"I'll review this with the town council." Eliza took the notepad with her as she stood. "Thank you, Lyra. You've given us a lot to consider. And if you get more signatures, you know where to find me."

As I left the room, Vex padded silently at my side. *One point for you. Zero for the glowering chief.*

I wasn't so sure.

We headed to the antique shop next.

Greer's Curiosities stood at the far end of a cobbled alley that always seemed colder than the rest of town, no matter the season. The storefront was crooked with age, its wooden shingles faded to a silver gray, and the bell above the door tinkled like wind chimes made of secrets.

Inside, the air was saturated with the scent of old leather, oil, and dust. Shelves overflowed with oddities—carved figurines, cracked mirrors, rusted keys, and ancient books. And at the center of it all was Samuel Greer.

He was a young man but old-fashioned and loved his antiques, right down to his clothing. He wore a navy waistcoat over a white button-down, his sleeves rolled to the elbows and arms inked with winding vines and arcane symbols. His hair was dark blond and slightly tousled, and his smile could've lit a room even if every bulb had blown. Although, he wasn't smiling at the moment.

He stood arguing with a woman I'd never seen.

"You can't keep ghosting me, Sammy." She tucked her shoulder-length pale brown hair behind her ears and then folded her hands in front of her simple A-line dress.

"For the millionth time, Evelyn, it's Samuel, and I'm not ghosting you." He threw his hands up. "I don't even know you, and you can be sure I never swiped right."

"I don't believe you. I swiped right, too, so that makes us a match. You can't undo that." She nodded once as if that made it a done deal. "I came all this way. You owe me a date."

"Look, I'm sorry. Truly I am, but someone is playing a terrible joke on you and me both, it seems. I neither have the time nor the inclination to date, and I never asked you to come to Wishville."

I cleared my throat, and both of them looked at me startled.

"Ms. Wells!" Samuel stepped out from behind a glass case full of compass rings and bone dice. "A pleasure, as always."

"We're not done here, Sammy." Evelyn looked down her nose at me suspiciously and then walked out the door.

"Who was that?" I gestured toward the door where Evelyn had disappeared.

Samuel sighed, dragging a hand through his tousled hair as he leaned against the counter filled with curiosities. "Evelyn Poe. Apparently, she's convinced we're star-crossed lovers because of some supposed match on a dating app. I've tried explaining that she must have the wrong guy, but she's...persistent."

"She seems like trouble." I frowned.

"You have no idea," Samuel grumbled, his voice filled with exasperation. "She tracked me down here, to Wishville of all places, as if this town doesn't have enough mysteries to deal with. I have my hands full keeping Marin Holloway at bay. She's constantly hounding me for a story for *The Wish Weekly* about my well theories. Now Evelyn wants to add her delusions of romance to the mix."

I raised an eyebrow, unable to suppress a grin. "Well, congratulations on making an impression with the ladies."

"Impression? More like an invitation for craziness," he replied with a dry laugh. "I'm not ready to share my theories with anyone just yet, and do I strike you as someone trying their luck on dating apps? Honestly, with my schedule, I barely have time to sleep, let alone swipe." His face pinched for a moment. "Women are fickle. Unpredictable. I'm done with them." He inhaled a cleansing breath and gestured at the antique shop, filled with a kaleidoscope of trinkets. "This place demands all my attention, and then some."

"I can see that." I glanced around the room. "You're looking...well-stocked."

He grinned. "What can I say? I can't stop collecting. Late nights and too many books send me on all sorts of adventures. There's so much to learn right here in town. Did you know there's a reference in the 1813 town almanac to a 'stone mouth that swallows stars'? I believe it's connected to the wishing well folklore."

My heart skipped a beat, but I smiled through it. "Most likely a poetic metaphor."

"Or," he said, stepping closer, "a portal."

Vex let out a low warning growl.

Samuel flinched. "Your cat hates me."

"He hates everyone," I said. "You're not special."

Samuel laughed, low and smooth. "I've missed our chats."

"Is that what you call them? You try to trap me in conversations about ancient artifacts, I deflect with dry wit, and you insist on offering me questionable tea."

He reached behind the counter and poured from a decanter. "Elderflower and mint this time. No bones."

"That's not reassuring."

We moved to the small sitting area near the fireplace, where a velvet fainting couch threatened to collapse under the next person's weight who sat on it. After a brief hesitation, I chose the chair next to it and sat stiffly, my fingers tracing the curve of my pendant, feeling as if I'd traveled back in time. The 1800s had been a special time for me. I smiled sadly. It made me miss my mother.

"What brings you in today?" he asked, handing me the tea.

I shook off my melancholy and glanced at the cup. I was more of a latte girl myself, but I took a cautious sip and blinked. It was surprisingly pleasant. "I'm here to ask you to sign a petition. The new police chief wants to reduce the frequency of WishFest."

Samuel's expression shifted subtly to something thoughtful and just a little disappointed. "That would be a shame. WishFest has...a heartbeat."

"That's what I said."

He reached for the new notepad I had brought to get more signatures and signed his name in a graceful, looping hand then handed it back.

"I appreciate your support," I said, rising.

He hesitated, then tilted his head. "Tell me something, Lyra. What do you believe the well *really* is?"

I blinked. "A symbol. A connection to history."

"Hmm."

"What?"

"You didn't say a myth."

I met his gaze evenly. "I choose not to speculate. The mystery of the well is what draws people to Wishville, and those quarterly wishes keep this town afloat."

"Yes," he murmured, staring off into space. "Some of us just dig a little deeper than wishes."

I placed my cup on the table and left before I could say something I'd regret. Outside, the wind shifted. And behind me, Samuel Greer stood in his doorway, sipping tea and staring after me like a man who already knew too much.

WISHFEST WAS STILL DAYS AWAY, but Wishville already buzzed with preparations. My job was to make sure the venders had everything they needed, book the entertainment, secure the food trucks, and provide the special wish tokens at the start of each festival.

The festival was so old, I hired a handyman, Eli Dunmore, to be on call for anything that broke down. He was tall, built like a lumberjack with thick black hair and beard, and skilled in just about everything.

So far, he'd proven to be a godsend. We couldn't afford any setbacks. The mayor had agreed that this spring WishFest was a go since so much prep work had already been done. It was the other seasons that were in question.

At this hour—just before dawn—the town belonged to the fog.

A cold snap had blown through last night, which wasn't unusual during early spring in Vermont. The streets were hushed, wrapped in a silvery mist that clung low to the ground. The lamp-posts along the square were still on faintly during pre-dawn, casting small halos of gold across damp cobblestones in our old-fashioned mountain town.

Even the birds had yet to stir.

I walked slowly, wearing my thicker spandex pants and long sleeve t-shirt today, my gloved hands buried in my sage green coat pockets and a beanie on my head. My boots crunched on the path, the spiral pendant around my neck warm against my chest.

Vex trotted ahead with purpose, his sleek black form weaving between the puddles like a shadow come to life. His eyes gleamed —today, one was a cool, reflective silver, the other a pale blue.

You know, he said through our bond, *there are warmer ways to get your morning steps in.*

"None as quiet." We didn't stop walking until we reached the forest clearing.

He paused by the wishing well and leaped onto the rim, his tail twitching. I followed, my boots tapping softly against the stone path. The well loomed at the edge of the clearing, older than the town itself. Covered in moss and lichen, its stones glistened with dew, and the iron grate that sealed the portal below glimmered faintly in the half-light. Only the incantation could make the grate vanish.

Or a break in the treaty.

The closer I got to the well, the ground pulsed beneath my feet. Not visibly—no vibration or sound—but a deep, rhythmic thrum I felt in my bones. It had been doing that more often lately. Trouble was coming. The kind you could only feel if you truly listened. That's when I heard the clatter. Glass on stone. A muffled curse.

From the back of a craft tent, a shape emerged—wrapped in mismatched layers of flannel and boots two sizes too big—dragging a red milk crate filled with clinking bottles.

"Stan?" I called softly.

Stan McDuff—Stan the Can, as everyone called him— paused, his hunched form bathed in flickering light from a lamppost ready to shut off for the day. His beard was more scruff than style, and his breath puffed white in the morning chill. He blinked at me, as if trying to place who—or *what*— I was.

Then he tilted his head and said, "The well don't like being watched."

My skin prickled. "What was that?"

He looked confused for a second, then shook his head. "Didn't say nothin'. Just bottles talkin', is all."

"Stan, what did you mean?"

He turned in a slow circle, one fingerless gloved hand pointing at the stones. "It's got an eye, that well does. An old eye. You look too long, it looks back. I seen it." He nodded. "Seen it move."

Vex let out a low warning growl.

Then Stan hiccupped, saluted Vex with a half-eaten granola bar, and wandered off into the mist, still mumbling to himself.

I turned to Vex. "File that under 'disturbing things to hear before sunrise.'"

That's a big file in this town.

I took a couple steps around the well, meaning to reassure myself, but then I saw him.

A dark figure slumped against the base. The mist parted just enough for the shape to take form. A man with limbs twisted unnaturally, head bowed forward, and one hand limp at his side. I covered my mouth with my hand, stifling my gasp.

Samuel Greer.

I rushed forward and dropped to my knees beside him. "Samuel?"

No response.

His skin was pale and waxy, his lips tinged with gray-blue. A jagged breath escaped me. "No. No, no, no." I touched his neck with my fingertips.

Cold. Still.

Vex padded up beside me. *He's gone, Lyra.*

I stared down at Samuel Greer—charming, curious, too-clever Samuel—the antique dealer who knew more than he let on. His waistcoat was damp from the cobblestones, one boot slightly untied.

And then the pendant at my neck vibrated. Hard. Hot. The

well answered, a low invisible thrum that buzzed through the soles of my boots.

"Something's wrong," I whispered.

Look, Vex said, his eyes locked on the moss behind Samuel's right hand. Strange burn marks were on some nearby vines and half-buried in the damp green was a glint of crystal—no larger than a robin's egg, its surface cracked and flickering faintly with inner light.

A memory crystal.

I gasped. How had he gotten one of those? I leaned forward and carefully pried it loose. It was warm in my hand. Too warm. As if it had been used recently—or was still trying to show something. I slipped it into my coat pocket just as a voice cut through the fog like a blade.

"Ms. Wells?"

I stood abruptly and turned.

Chief Holden Thorn emerged from the mist, his trademark sport coat billowing open, revealing his shoulder harness and gun, his expression hard and sharp. He moved with the precision of a man used to emergencies—his stormy eyes already assessing the scene as his hand hovered near the radio at his hip.

When his gaze landed on Samuel's body, I saw the flicker of recognition. And when they found me again, there was something else layered beneath the suspicion.

Concern maybe?

"What happened?" he asked, his voice low and urgent as he stepped forward and crouched beside Samuel. Holden's hand moved with practiced care—checking his pulse, examining his eyes, his mouth. Then he exhaled. "No visible injuries, except his eyes look a little weird, cloudy," he murmured. "Could be cardiac arrest. Or poisoning." He glanced up at me. "Are you all right?"

I hated the way my breath hitched over his concern. Hated the flicker of warmth that rose in my chest at the sound of that voice—steady, graveled, infuriatingly grounding.

"I—I was walking Vex." I swallowed hard. "And I found Mr. Greer like this."

"Did you see anyone else?"

"Just Stan," I said, "but he was...rambling incoherently. Something about the well watching him."

Holden's gaze flicked toward the well, then back to me. "And what do *you* think?"

My fingers curled tightly over the edge of my coat pocket, where the crystal burned. "I think a tragic accident must have happened."

"That remains to be seen." His gaze narrowed on me. "The festival hasn't even started, and we already have trouble." He stood slowly, towering over me in the fog. "I'll need a statement, and we'll need the medical examiner."

Vex slinked closer to my ankle. *Tell him.*

I didn't move.

"Lyra," Holden said more gently, "are you sure you're okay?"

"I'm fine," I replied quickly.

His eyes searched mine. Not just for lies, but for truths I wasn't ready to share.

He didn't believe me, not fully, but he nodded and reached for his radio. "This is Chief Thorn. I've got a 10-79 at the wishing well. One male, no obvious trauma. Name is Samuel Greer. Requesting backup and the medical examiner."

His voice faded into the mist as I looked down at Samuel's still form. Did he die of natural causes? Or did whatever he had uncovered—whatever secrets he'd brushed up against—kill him?

The well had given *me* the clue, but I couldn't help thinking it came with a price.

And then, through the mist, a shrill voice cried, "Lyra! The ghosts are assembling! I knew it!" Dot barreled onto the scene, her polka dots damp from the fog, holding her oversized mug in one hand and a weather-beaten book in the other. "This mist? It's not weather...it's a veil. And behind it, a ghost army waits for judgment."

I groaned softly. "Dottie—"

Before I could finish, Belle clattered in behind her, with sequins damp and pigeons fluttering from her shawl. "Oh please, I predicted this death three weeks ago when my mirror cracked and formed the shape of a tragic face."

"You predicted a moldy apple," Tilly corrected, limping up last with a determined expression. "I wrote in my journal that someone would die near a compass. Greer's whole shop is filled with them. That counts."

The three began bickering loudly.

Police officers who had arrived on the scene exchanged helpless looks.

Thorn looked like he might arrest all three on principle.

Belle, still shouting about spiritual omens, pointed at the well. "That well is humming. That's not normal, honey. Even I know that."

She was right. The vibration wasn't sound. It was magical resonance.

"It's just old, Belle." I edged closer to the well with my heart pounding, ignoring Thorn's glare as I looked over the side and pressed my palm against the rim.

It pulsed in time with the memory crystal hidden inside my pocket.

By the time I gave my statement to Chief Thorn and returned home, the sky had fully brightened into a pale, indifferent blue. The kind of morning that looked clean and calm but carried the weight of things unsaid. The path leading up to my father's old house twisted through birch trees still slick from the dawn's chill. Their bark peeled like old parchment, revealing pale veins beneath.

I unlatched the iron gate and walked up the stone steps. Vex trailed behind me in silence, his tail low, his ears swiveling. The moment I stepped inside, I turned the bolt on the door with a *click*. The sound echoed louder than it should have.

Home, but it didn't feel that way today.

The air inside was cool and shadowed. Morning light sliced through the room in yellow rays, and dust motes spun in the beams. I shrugged off my coat and hung it in the closet. Then I took a breath and pulled the memory crystal from my pocket. It was warm, still vibrating faintly with an energy that didn't belong to me.

Cracked through the middle, but holding on the way I was.

Vex leaped onto the table and padded closer, his eyes fixed on the shard. His voice slid into my thoughts like a whisper behind my ear. *The past is leaking, and it doesn't like to be ignored.*

Because Dwellers lived beneath the well and near the Earth's hidden layers, their powers were tied to subterranean elements—water tables, magma flows, and the planet's inner energy. As the only half-human, half-Dweller, I bridged above ground elements like air, light, and celestial forces with subterranean ones like water, magma and core, giving me powers that no full Dweller or human could access.

"What does that mean, the past is leaking?" I squinted at him. "And you can speak, you know. No one is around."

"In time you will know," he said out loud and then jumped down.

I shrugged. Vex could be mysterious at times. I focused on the crystal, its fractured glow throwing spiderweb shadows across the old table. My fingers tingled as I turned it over in my hand.

"I shouldn't have this," I said softly. "Calderis would be livid if he knew a human had it by the well."

Vex flicked his tail, unimpressed. "When is he *not* livid?"

"I would understand if he was." I nodded. "This could start something if it fell into the wrong hands." I turned the crystal again, watching how the crack caught the light. "He'll say I've overstepped. That I've broken trust. That I should have brought it to him right away."

"But you didn't."

"No."

I crossed to the bookshelf near the fireplace and pulled down a narrow tin box carved with ancient Dweller runes. Inside was the copper dish—smooth and shallow, etched with spiral script, and set with a ring of quartz along the rim.

A memory lens.

My mother had used it once, a lifetime ago. I brought it to the table and placed it between us.

Vex circled once, then sat, and folded his paws. "You could still turn it in."

I shook my head. "Not yet. The Council of Elders doesn't trust me to do my job. They really won't if they find out about Samuel's death. I need to figure out what happened to him first and make sure WishFest still goes on. We've never had a murder during the festival. I can't risk this putting a crack in the treaty. If the chosen one's wish doesn't get granted this season, then the treaty will be broken for sure."

Keeping the lights off, I reached for the candle on the windowsill, lit it with a match, and let the warm light spill across the table. Then, carefully, I placed the crystal in the center of the lens. The runes glowed faintly in response, recognizing the magic. The crystal began to vibrate. A shimmer rippled through the air like heat rising off stone. The pendant at my neck glowed in answer.

I whispered the incantation.

It came easy, even after all these years. Ancient language sliding over my tongue like water over river stones. The copper dish vibrated once, then the air above it shifted—bent inward— and from the fractured crystal, light unfurled.

The memory shimmered to life.

Samuel appeared, rendered in flickering light and sound. He stood at the wishing well, moonlight glinting off his waistcoat buttons, his expression full of restless curiosity. He looked younger, somehow.

More vulnerable.

"They won't tell me." His voice echoed faintly around the room. "But I know it's not just legend. The stories match too closely. The dreams. The pull. The water tastes different..." He kneeled on the ground, one hand brushing along the base of the well—almost lovingly. "I saw her vanish in there once. Lyra. She thought I wasn't looking."

My stomach dropped.

"She's the key. She knows more than she says. There has to be a portal. Magic. And it's guarded."

The memory flickered.

A blur passed through the frame—fast. Shadowy.

Samuel's head jerked toward the sound. "Hello?"

No response.

He stood, turned, and faced something just beyond the well. His mouth opened, as if to speak again—but then came a voice. Sharp. Hollow.

"What have you done? You went too far this time."

The memory ended in a crackle of light.

Another memory started to form, but Samuel wasn't in it. I needed to process this information, so I snatched the crystal off the dish, vowing to go back and listen to the other memories when I was ready.

The crystal dimmed, and the copper dish stopped glowing.

Silence.

Except for my breath, ragged in my throat. Vex's fur was puffed out along his spine.

"What did he do, and what did he go too far with?" I whispered, looking at Vex. "Taking the memory crystal? Finding the truth behind the well? Or something else that has to do with Wishville?"

"And who didn't want their secrets revealed," Vex added darkly.

I stared at the place where the memory had just been. The glow had left a faint ring on the table's surface, like a ghost mark. That voice...it could have been either human or Dweller, and it was impossible to tell if it was male or female.

"Tell me you saw it." I slipped the memory crystal into my pocket before standing and pacing the room. "That shadow behind him?"

"Yes."

"Samuel Greer didn't die of natural causes...he was murdered," I said, my voice barely a whisper. There were many types of crystals in Elarion. Memory crystals recorded what was happening to the person who held it, but they were fragile and could be damaged easily.

Vex looked up at me, his gaze unsettlingly calm. "Then it's already begun."

"What do you mean?"

"I heard from my sources that Samuel got a hold of a wish token somehow and made a wish before the festival started, which as you know is forbidden."

"Oh, no. How did he get a wish token?"

"Probably the same way he got a memory crystal."

"This whole situation is worse than I thought." I sank into the rocking chair, the old wood creaking under me, and my hands shook. I pressed the pendant flat against my sternum, trying to still the wild flutter of my heart. I had always known the treaty was fragile, but this wasn't just cracks forming in the agreement between humans and Dwellers.

This was an actual break I might not be able to fix.

"You should tell Calderis," Vex said gently. "Maybe the crack can be repaired and a wish recipient can still be chosen in time."

I nodded slowly. "I will, but I need to know more first. I need to know *who* that was—human or Dweller—and why they were near the well."

"Careful or you might be the next target!"

I met his eyes. "Then they'd better come prepared."

The air shifted again, and the flame in the candle sputtered out. I flicked the lights back on. Outside, the wind howled through the trees like it knew something I didn't, and in my pocket, the broken crystal pulsed once more...

Like a heartbeat of knowledge that refused to be silenced.

CHAPTER
Six

THE NEXT MORNING *Town Hall* smelled like lemon polish, perfume, and deodorant. The meeting room was packed wall-to-wall, every folding chair filled, every inch of the cream-painted walls vibrating with anxious chatter.

Someone brought muffins.

Someone else brought their emotional support ferret.

Mayor Hemsworth sat at the head of the long table in her red cardigan, her hands folded before her. Next to her, Assistant Mayor Delaney fiddled nervously with a stack of papers, his comb-over looking dangerously close to airborne.

The hall buzzed with anticipation, the kind of tightly coiled energy that suggested something important was about to either be decided—or explode. I slipped in quietly, with Vex perched on my shoulder like a silky gargoyle. The meeting hadn't started yet, but the front row had already been claimed, unsurprisingly, by the Wellies.

Tilly sat ramrod straight, her patchwork skirt overflowing into the next seat, clutching her infamous journal. "Page seventy-three," she announced to no one in particular. "Sharp pain in the lower left side. I told you something was going to rupture—societally."

Beside her, Belle sparkled in full sequins, a feathered shawl draped across her shoulders, as she scribbled "Magical Defense Committee" onto a volunteer signup sheet she'd apparently made herself. "If the mayor won't form a task force, I will. I shall chair it, obviously. The pigeons and I are ready."

On the other side, Dot passed around her floral teacup. "Sip and tell, everyone," she cooed. "If you get goosebumps, it means you're part of the prophecy."

People gave them a wide berth—but no one dared ask them to leave.

The mayor stood and took her spot at the podium then cleared her throat loudly. "Let's come to order."

The Wellies did not.

Chief Thorn entered with his usual scowl, his hands hovering near his hips as if he were bracing for battle. His eyes narrowed the instant they landed on the trio. "Are they officially on the docket?" he muttered under his breath as he passed me, clearly talking to himself.

"You'd have to ask the tea leaves," I couldn't resist murmuring back, but he didn't hear me.

He came to a stop beside the mayor and crossed his arms, his jaw tightening. He wore his sport coat, shirt, and tie like a second skin—all authority and stormy eyes. He glanced once at me across the crowd, and I hated how the contact made my stomach flutter.

The meeting began—reassurances that Samuel's death was being fully investigated, but the festival was a go. Talks proceeded about festival budgets, patrol resources, increased tourism—and then veered off the rails entirely when the Wellies interjected their wisdom.

Belle stood and declared, "I move to enchant the town perimeter. Just as a precaution. Maybe a protective rune or two. I have chalk."

Tilly raised her journal high. "My spleen says the veil is thinning!"

Dot's teacup rattled ominously as she whispered, "The mist speaks...and it says someone among us has secrets."

The mayor massaged her temples. "Ladies, please—"

Thorn looked ready to move to another state.

I almost laughed—almost.

But then Tilly muttered, "There's something wrong near the well. Not just the magic...but memory. Like something's missing."

That chilled me. She couldn't possibly know about the veil thinning or the memory crystal. The Wellies might be eccentric, loud, and frequently incorrect—but occasionally, they were terrifyingly close to the truth. I sat up straighter because, if they were feeling it...then the danger wasn't coming.

It was already here.

Trip Danderly raised a hand from the third row, his glittery badge sparkling as it caught the overhead light. "Chief! As Wishville's self-appointed Wish Sheriff, I demand to be officially deputized for the duration of this investigation. I brought my wand." He whipped it out of the holster at his waist. "It glows."

Chief Thorn didn't even blink. "Trip, we've talked about this. Several times. Please put your wand-flashlight away."

Trip huffed and sat but not before blowing imaginary dust from the tip of his wand, twirling it in his hand, and then expertly sliding it into a holster. "I'll be over here if justice needs me."

Eliza cleared her throat, drawing the room's attention like a conductor raising her baton. "Folks, thank you for coming. Chief Thorn and his officers have the investigation of Samuel Greer's death under control. I expect you all to fully cooperate with whatever the chief needs as well as do your part to make the festival a success."

Whispers rippled like silk through the crowd.

"Sam tripped, didn't he?" Maisie Flint said with her arms crossed. She owned *The General Store* and had a photographic memory. "I told him not to walk that slippery moss in those slick shoes. He should have listened to his elders."

"He was researching crazy conspiracy theories, pointing out

odd scorched vines near the well, sticking his nose in places it didn't belong. Heck, he probably made those scorch marks himself, trying to make the well more than it is," muttered Rowan Baxter from the back. Rowan was the town historian and caretaker of the wishing well monument.

Reed Callahan, an inventor and clockmaker, added, "I caught him snooping in my workshop, looking for temperature tracking mechanisms to detect magical activity. Sounds to me like he got too close to the crazy."

"More like too close to the edge," added self-proclaimed wish coach, Glenda Fernweather, as she fanned her bottle-blonde hair with a mini rhinestone-studded vision board. "That moss is a death trap. I've been complaining about it for years. He probably fell."

Doctor Oliver Greaves stood up near the front, his medical bag on the floor beside him. "If I may...Samuel was in my office less than a week ago. Routine check-up and full bloodwork. Without saying too much, I can assure you he had no signs of heart trouble or underlying conditions. He was healthy and not likely to faint or fall."

Chief Thorn stepped forward. "The Medical Examiner's early report said there were no signs of a struggle other than his twisted limbs, but that could have just been how he fell. There were no footprints or drag marks and no obvious cause of death like cardiac arrest or poison."

More murmurs.

Someone gasped.

Someone else dropped a muffin.

"So, you're saying a young, healthy person can just drop dead for no reason?" Willa Hartman, owner of *The Wishbone Café*, asked, her voice sharp as a steak knife. Willa lived for gossip. "Sounds suspicious to me."

Chief Thorn scanned the room. "I didn't say it wasn't suspicious. Even the M.E. said it was odd. No visible signs of trauma except for a few cold exposure symptoms, but we did have a cold snap last night. Until we know more, I'm treating it as a potential crime."

Trip stood again, adjusting his flashlight like it was a badge of honor. "This sounds like wish tampering! Or maybe sabotage! Sabo-wish?"

"Trip," the chief warned.

"All I'm saying," Trip continued, undeterred, "is I've got excellent instincts, and I watched three seasons of 'Murder Most Magical.' I know how these things go."

I pressed my fingers to my pendant. The silver spiral was cool against my skin, the metal attuned to the well's ancient magic. I could still feel the echo of Samuel's presence—and something else. Something older.

Something to do with my mother maybe.

"Samuel was searching for something," Willa said. "He told me he had news that would shock everyone. Didn't he go to see you a while back, Lyra?"

Everyone turned to look at me.

Even the ferret looked alarmed.

"Yes," I confirmed, keeping my voice calm and my eyes from looking at Holden. "Since I'm a member of the Historical Society and chair of WishFest, he wanted my opinion on the well and the Folklore. He said he believed there was more to the stories than people thought, which there isn't, of course. There's no proof that it's anything more than a legend."

"Samuel came to see you?" Chief Thorn's words drew my gaze. He narrowed his eyes. "You didn't think to tell me this earlier?"

I lifted my chin, barely remembering that visit since it had been a while ago. "I didn't think it was relevant." Besides, I didn't want to give him another reason to cancel WishFest. That *legend* was a necessity for Wishville.

His eyes darkened, but he said nothing.

"Samuel was so desperate to find proof that Elarion and Dwellers exist like the old folklore tales suggest," I turned back to the crowd, "that he began to spiral, and now he's gone. We all have fun with the legend of the magical wishing well, but it isn't healthy for anyone to become obsessed with it."

"Oh honey, most of us know those fairy tales aren't real, but there's always a few diehard fanatics who believe the lost city of Elarion actually exists somewhere," Magnolia McHoggin, owner of *Blooms of Glory*, said from her seat near the exit, a black veil perched on her head like she was mourning a particularly beloved begonia. Ever since I could remember, she had staged funerals for every dead flower in her shop. "Do you really think Samuel was murdered? Maybe he was onto something else and someone silenced him."

"We don't know anything yet," Eliza interjected calmly, folding her hands tighter. "Chief Thorn will keep us all informed."

A hand shot up. Bartholomew Gildersnipe, the butcher who owned *Boar's Board and Brisket*, wore an apron decorated with pictures of his pet pig named Trotter. "Can we still hold all the WishFest activities? I already ordered my patriotic brisket bunting."

"And my hot air balloon is ready to go," Weylan, the tour guide with piercing green eyes, said, his dark blond hair brushing his shoulders. He was new to this year's festival. "It cost a lot to operate these things you, know. We all count on these festivals." His gaze briefly met mine before looking away.

My forehead puckered.

"It's still on the calendar," Eliza said, "but the town council will meet again tonight to discuss any changes."

"No changes!" barked Gus, twirling his handlebar mustache. "This town needs tradition now more than ever. We cancel Wish-Fest, we cancel hope."

"He's right," I said with conviction. "We need to preserve the history of the well and keep it going. The people have spoken."

Holden gave me a long, unreadable look.

He didn't say anything more, but I could see the gears turning behind his eyes. Suspicion, calculation, and something else I couldn't name. I was the last person to talk to Samuel. I was the one who had found him. I had a reason to want to silence his crazy theories. I had told Holden that Stan was there, but Stan didn't remember a thing because he'd been sleepwalking after a night of over-indulging, making me look even more suspicious.

Behind me, the hall buzzed louder than ever, a hive of questions with no queen to answer them. I could still feel Holden's eyes on my back, his scrutiny prickling my nerves. And somewhere deep inside me, that thrum returned—the one that said nothing in Wishville ever stayed buried for long. The truth always came out, but what truth? The truth of Samuel's death, or the truth about the well?

That was a truth I needed to stay hidden at any cost.

The fluorescent lights in Chief Thorn's office buzzed faintly, as if they too were suspicious of me. The room was all sterile grays and navy blues—bare walls, a desk that looked too heavy to move, and a single window with partially drawn blinds. A coffee mug sat on his desk, emblazoned with the words "Justice Never Sleeps." The scent of paper, ink, and strong coffee hung in the air.

I sat in a chair that was far too hard, the vinyl seat cracked along the edge, my hands curled in my lap.

Across from me, Chief Holden Thorn didn't sit. He stood with his arms folded and one shoulder leaning against the doorframe like he was giving me the illusion of casual calm. But everything about him was taut—from the sharp line of his jaw to the way his eyes watched me like a hawk sighting prey.

Outside the window, the street looked deceptively peaceful. The flower shop's hanging baskets swayed in the breeze, and a pair of teenagers zipped past on skateboards. Life in Wishville carried on.

Inside, everything felt like it was closing in.

"Given the new information you mentioned in the town hall meeting, I asked you here to go over your story again. Let's start from the beginning," Holden said, his voice calm but clipped. "You found Samuel at the well. Around what time?"

I met his gaze. "Just before dawn, maybe five-fifteen. I walk Vex early. It's when the town is quiet."

"I still can't believe you walk your cat." He jotted something in a small leather notebook, his pen making short, decisive strokes. "And you were alone?"

"No. Like I said earlier, Stan McDuff was there." I kept my voice firm and steady. "He was sleep-sorting bottles again after a bender. He saw me, but he doesn't remember."

Holden arched an eyebrow. "Stan McDuff also thought his recycling bin was speaking Latin and couldn't remember his own middle name this morning."

"He does that sometimes." I shook my head and threw my hands up. "That doesn't mean he didn't see me."

"It means," Holden said slowly, "that there are no reliable witnesses to corroborate your story."

I clenched my fingers tighter. "You think I killed Samuel. How? You said it yourself. There were no obvious causes other than a cold night. Besides, what would I possibly gain by jeopardizing WishFest?"

Holden didn't answer right away. He stepped forward, circled the desk, and leaned both hands on its edge, the light above catching on the faint scar through his eyebrow.

"I think," he said carefully, "that you were one of the last people to see him alive. A young, healthy man with no obvious medical issues, and now he's dead."

I blew out a frustrated sigh. "Maybe there's something we can't see. Something the final autopsy report will show."

"Maybe you're right." His eyes narrowed. "Maybe something you and your Wellies slipped him."

"Those women are eccentric but not evil."

"And yet," Holden said, straightening, "Samuel's crazy theories about the well show how dangerous WishFest can be, which you're all so adamant to preserve. The question is, how far would you go to protect the legend of the well and keep the festival alive?"

"Those little old ladies aren't capable of hurting a flea."

"They don't have to. They have you." His gaze held mine. "What exactly are *you* capable of, Ms. Wells?"

My temper flared. I stood abruptly, the chair scraping back across the tile with an angry squeal. "This is ridiculous. If you're looking for suspects, maybe start with the people who actually had issues with Samuel."

"Like who?"

I began to pace, needing motion to release the energy surging through me. "What about this Evelyn Poe woman?" I pressed. "She's not even from Wishville. She was stalking Samuel, obsessed with him. Trust me when I say he did not feel the same. And don't get me started on Marin Holloway. She would do anything to get *the scoop* for the paper, but Samuel wasn't cooperating."

"Trust *me*. I plan to look into several people, but right now, we're talking about you," Holden said coolly. "And your lack of an alibi after midnight."

I turned on him. "I live alone, Chief, with no neighbors. Just my cat. And I wasn't planning on having to prove my innocence when I took a morning walk!"

His jaw tensed. "This isn't an accusation, Ms. Wells. This is procedure." He frowned. "You really should have security cameras, living so remote."

"What can I say, I'm old-fashioned."

His voice softened, "Old-fashioned can get you killed, Lyra. Maybe it's time to modernize."

I blinked over his use of my first name, then cleared my throat. "My father's house is old." I shrugged. "I was planning to renovate it soon." I paused a beat then swiped my hand through the air as I glared at him. "Why do you care about my safety when you're treating me like a suspect?"

He ran a hand over his rigid bearded jaw and sighed. "I'm treating everyone like a suspect until the evidence proves otherwise."

"That's convenient," I said bitterly.

He stepped toward me, just enough to fill the space between us, but not enough to crowd me. The scent of smoky cedar and leather, with a hint of Bourbon, clung to him. His voice softened again. "It's my job to be observant, Lyra. I see how this town looks at you."

That stopped me. My lips parted, but no words came out.

"You're a mystery to them," he continued. "You're friendly enough, yet you keep to yourself, just out of reach. Too calm. Too quiet. Too *alone*. And now Samuel Greer, the town's favorite eccentric antique dealer, ends up dead on your morning route."

I swallowed past the lump in my throat. He'd touched a nerve. I wanted more than anything to have human friends, but our differences led to questions I was forbidden to answer. Inevitably, I had to erase their memories and start over. And eventually, by my own death, I would lose my Dweller friends as well.

Being a half-blood made for a very lonely existence.

So, I protected my heart and kept my distance from everyone except Vex. He was me in animal form, and the only one who understood what it was like. Hence the reason he was so *vexed* all the time.

"I didn't hurt Samuel, Holden," I responded. "I found him. That's all."

Holden studied me for a long moment. Then, finally, he nodded and walked back around to his chair, sitting for the first time. The authority didn't drain from him, but something less rigid slipped into his posture.

"What did you see when you found him? *Exactly*."

I lowered myself back into the chair, slower this time. "He was slumped against the well. His head leaned to one side. I thought he was asleep until I felt for a pulse."

Holden scribbled something else. "Was anything out of place?"

I hesitated. My fingers grazed my pendant again. "The air felt wrong. Still. Heavy. Like the moment before a thunderstorm."

He looked up with an arched brow. "Okay...anything *physical*?"

"Oh, right." Sometimes I forgot which realm I was in. "No. Just him. No one else around."

Holden leaned back, and his chair creaked. "You can leave," he said quietly, "but stay in town."

"Where else would I go, Chief? Wishville is my home. I wouldn't dream of leaving." I stood once again and reached for the door, my hand closing around the cool brass knob.

"Lyra," he said.

I paused with my back to him. "Yes?"

"If you remember anything else—anything that seems strange, even if it doesn't make sense—I need to know."

I didn't turn around. "Of course." And then I stepped out into the hallway, the fluorescent lights fading behind me. The station lobby was quiet. Worn chairs lined the wall, and a rack of flyers for bake sales and lost pets fluttered slightly in the breeze from the door. I pushed outside into the crisp air. The sun was warmer now, but I still felt cold.

From knowing I was running out of time.

A wish needed to be granted this season, or the treaty would be broken and war would inevitably resume. Someone in this town—someone who might be watching me right now—had decided Samuel Greer knew too much.

Maybe they would decide the same about me.

CHAPTER
Seven

SPRING.

The celebration of the end of winter and a burst of new life. Fresh, local and maple kissed was the theme, highlighting Wishville's agricultural heritage, farm-to-table culture and New England charm.

WishFest had officially begun, whether Chief Thorn liked it or not.

Colorful banners fluttered along Main Street, directing festival goers up the cobblestone path to the clearing in the forest where the festival took place around the wishing well. Vendors hawked everything from enchanted trinkets to maple-glazed pulled pork sliders and strawberry rhubarb crisp. The townspeople tried to pretend everything was perfectly fine.

It wasn't.

Samuel Greer's death had left a hollow in the heart of town, even if no one said it out loud. Chief Thorn was neck-deep in the investigation, and while he didn't have the authority to outright forbid the festival, I knew the furrow between his brows had deepened when he saw the wishing well glittering like a magician's main act.

Food trucks, vender tents, games, rides, a hot air balloon and more would last for a week, until everyone had placed their wish in the well, and then one lucky recipient would see their wish come true.

Providing the well could choose a wish recipient in time.

I still had to talk to Calderis, but first, I needed to make sure the opening ceremonies went off without a hitch. I stood on the fringe of the crowd, with Vex perched on my shoulder. His tail flicked in disapproval as Betsy, in her bread apron, tossed dried sage into the air and shouted something vaguely mystical about aligning moonlight with gluten.

"This is what passes for ritual now?" Vex murmured, his voice laced with disdain. "I've seen more convincing summoning circles made out of cereal."

"It's theater," I said. "They need normalcy, or the illusion of it."

"It's idiocy," he corrected, "and poor form. That woman is waving a cinnamon stick like it's a scepter of power."

Maisie had set up a booth under the old birch tree, her table cluttered with neon charms in the shape of bones, teeth, and what I was fairly certain was a glow-in-the-dark duck foot from her general store. She wore her long, gray hair in a bun and dark sunglasses to protect her precious eyes and photographic memory.

"Glow in the dark bone charms! Wards against bad wishes!" she cried, shaking a small pouch of what looked suspiciously like glow stick powder.

I sighed. Totally fake, but people seemed to love them.

On the makeshift stage, Assistant Mayor Delaney adjusted his microphone. "And now, for our opening ceremony, the illustrious Glenda Fernweather will perform the Summoning of Spirits!"

Someone near the stage whooped.

Someone else groaned.

Vex dug his claws deeper into my scarf.

Glenda swept onto the stage like a bottle-blond tornado, her velvet robes trailing behind her, holding a wand made from a bedazzled curtain rod raised high. The crowd hushed as she twirled three times, shouted something in fake Latin that sounded suspiciously like a pasta order, and then promptly swooned.

"Oh heavens, the spirits have taken me!" She flopped onto the stage like a dying swan in community theater, one arm flung dramatically over her face.

"Not again," someone muttered behind me.

The assistant mayor clapped politely, clearly unsure whether to call an ambulance or let her finish. A child in the front row offered her a juice box. Eli Dunmore helped her off the stage and then fixed a loose floorboard.

"That woman once tried to summon a parking spot and passed out on the sidewalk," Vex whispered.

"To be fair, she got the spot." I turned away from the drama, my attention snagging on movement in the mist beyond the well. The layer of morning fog thickened at the edge of the woods, curling around the tree trunks. For a heartbeat, the hairs on my arms lifted.

Someone was watching.

And then I saw him.

A silhouette at first. Broad shoulders, a purposeful gait, the glint of something metallic on his hip. The crowd moved around him without noticing, parting instinctively, unaware. He was dressed like a mechanic—worn jeans, grease-smudged shirt, fake tattoos, and cap pulled low over long, pale blond hair—but I knew those electric blue eyes.

Sparks.

My pulse stumbled like it missed a step. He shouldn't be here.

Sparks had been banished from Elarion to the outskirts of the realm years ago, stripped of his title, his voice in the Council, his name forbidden from being spoken aloud in the Dweller courts. He'd questioned the old laws, pushed back against the treaty—his rebellion had gotten him exiled.

I started to wave, but Vex growled low in his throat. "Don't make a scene. Not here."

"He crossed the line between worlds." I lowered my voice for his ears only.

"Yes, and we need to find out why before you go charging in like a heroine with a death wish," he hissed.

A ginger cat hopped onto the edge of the well, startling us both, stretching like she owned the place. Her tail swished once, twice, with eyes the color of honey fixed on Vex.

"Fenrin?" Vex said with a mix of surprise and fondness, if I wasn't mistaken.

Since when was Vex fond of anything?

The ginger cat dipped her head, feline politeness disguising something much deeper. Fenrin was no ordinary cat. She was a full Whispen and wasn't supposed to be in Wishville, either. The crack in the treaty was growing bigger. Had she come to warn us?

She blinked once, then looked past us.

"She sees him too," I murmured.

"Then we're not imagining it," Vex said. "He's really here."

Sparks moved with precision, slipping behind Maisie's booth and vanishing down the path into town. My feet moved before my brain could protest.

"Lyra," Vex warned.

"I won't make a scene," I said. "I just want to know what he's doing here."

I didn't stop moving until I reached the alley beside the auto-body shop, *Wishville Wheels*. The alley smelled like maple cream donuts, engine oil, and poorly made decisions. My boots crunched over broken plastic and discarded glitter wands. It always took at least a week to clean up after WishFest. The humans in this town were notorious for not caring about the earth.

You would never see trash scattered about Elarion.

I pressed myself to the corner of the building and peeked around.

Sparks stood with his back to me, inspecting the engine of an old pickup truck. He wiped his hands on a rag, glanced skyward, and muttered something in the old tongue. He turned slightly, and I saw the line of his jaw, the scar on his temple—a reminder of his last crossing into the human world. Not many remembered the riot at the edge of the veil, but I did.

I remembered everything.

Sparks was a wild card—younger, less controlled, and unpredictable. He could channel electrical energy through his hands, enough to jolt machinery, shock opponents, and restart broken devices.

Then he turned fully, and his eyes lit up with a sudden, startling blue. And light. Electric blue surged through his irises like twin storms, and small sparks danced around his fingertips. Static clung to the air around him. I could feel it in my teeth.

He was charged...literally.

"You can come out," he said without looking. "Your breathing gives you away."

I stepped into view. "You shouldn't be here."

When humans entered Elarion, their eyes and hair brightened and moved. The same went for Dwellers. When they exited Elarion, the reverse happened. They were still tall and attractive, but could definitely pass as human if one didn't know the subtleties to look for.

He smiled faintly. "Neither should you, technically. You are half-Dweller, yet here you are."

I folded my arms. "How are you in Wishville? Especially during WishFest? You didn't have anything to do with Samuel's murder did you?"

He looked past me, sparks flickering from his fingertips and vanishing into the damp air. "Rumor has it your friend Samuel stole a wish token and made an unauthorized wish before the festival began. That's forbidden. That wish cracked something open in the portal."

A chill wrapped around me, thicker than the fog, confirming my suspicions. "You're saying you didn't mean to come here?"

He shook his head. "Not at first. I felt it like a magnetic pull.

Raw kinetic energy bleeding through the veil. And I wasn't the only one who felt it."

I thought of Fenrin. "You think others crossed too?"

"I know they did," his electric eyes sizzled, "and not all of them have good intentions."

My heart thudded. "Do you think Samuel's killer could be a Dweller?"

"Possibly." Sparks's eyes dimmed, the lightning ebbing to a low, warning glow. "Or a human wielding knowledge of our realm they shouldn't have. We don't know for sure, and that's the danger. Samuel Greer knew too much. Who's to say another human didn't as well?" He turned and placed his hand on the rusted truck hood. A quiet hum filled the alley, and then a blue pulse of energy danced along the metal like a living current.

The truck sparked and coughed to life.

"You have to leave," I said, even though my voice sounded weak.

Sparks looked back, serious now. "No, I have to stay. Because if more cracks form, Elarion won't just be exposed—it'll be invaded. And if humans fall into our world..." He let the silence finish that thought, but I knew what he had wanted to say.

History would repeat itself.

"You got exiled out of Elarion." I studied him. "Why do you care about protecting it now?"

"Because I've been to other realms and have seen what happens when peace is broken. People get greedy and war destroys everyone."

"I can fix this," I said.

"It's not as easy as you think, Lyra." And with that, Sparks vanished into the mist before I could stop him.

I had to talk to Calderis. My job was to ensure WishFest took place each season. Now that Samuel made an unauthorized wish and then died, I wasn't sure what needed to happen for a wish recipient to be chosen and their wish fulfilled in order to close the crack in the well and keep the peace.

How hard could it be?

I slowly made my way back up the hill to the festival grounds in time to see Glenda being fanned by three high schoolers and Maisie handing a child a charm shaped like a chicken foot. The illusion of safety was intact, but the cracks beneath it were growing wider. I wasn't sure how much longer I could hold both worlds together.

Naturally, the Wellies had claimed the booth nearest the well.

Tilly sat behind a riot of tiny spell jars, each labeled with specific intentions: "Forget Regret," "Summon the Truth," and "Spleen Soother." She wore a patchwork vest over a blouse covered in embroidered herbs and muttered to people passing by things like, "This one vibrated when I sealed it. That means it's fate. Or gas. Hard to say."

Belle was on parade duty, draped in sequins that matched the metallic thread in her banner sash, and two pigeons perched on her shoulders cooing in rhythm. With dramatic flair, she waved a silver bell wand. "Welcome to the Spring Equinox Spectacular! Featuring drama, destiny, and discounted dreamcatchers!"

"Did she rehearse that?" Vex asked from under the edge of the maple cotton candy cart.

"I think she dreamed it," I replied.

Dot had set up shop behind a velvet curtain in the third corner of their shared booth. Her sign read: *Tea Truths—Sip If You Dare.* Most people dared. Inside, she poured floral blends into antique china, muttering things like, "Mmm, yes...a shadow around your love line. Could be a ghost. Could be heartburn."

When I peeked inside, Dot glanced up and whispered, "Did you know Magnolia is not who she says she is? I've been sensing royal energy. Mark my words, she's a princess in disguise."

I blinked. "Magnolia McHoggins, the florist?"

She nodded solemnly. "Or maybe it's the scrapbooker. My senses blur after lunch."

As I walked away, laughing under my breath, Tilly called out, "Oh, Lyra! Someone asked for a charm against veiling magic.

Said their memories keep slipping. Said something about needing a memory crystal, whatever that is. I told him I didn't carry those."

My heart skipped.

"Who asked?" I turned too fast.

Tilly blinked. "Didn't get a name. His eyes were like lightning, though, all sparks and fire. In fact, I've seen a few strange characters in town. Then again, WishFest has always brought out the wackos."

Belle clucked. "I for one love the wackos, and we could use a little more sparks and fire to liven up this festival."

"I've got a tea for that." Dot winked.

I stared at them.

The Wellies smiled, oblivious, waving at a group of children who passed by. The hair on the back of my neck stood up. The Wellies weren't magical, not technically, but they were circling too close to the truth.

And maybe just maybe...they weren't as oblivious as they looked.

The air had shifted by the time Vex and I made our way back down the wooded hill toward town. The makeshift trail that connected the festival grounds to the town square shimmered with lights strung between trees, casting an amber glow on the path below. Laughter drifted down from the clearing, mingling with fiddle music, the smell of roasted nuts, and a cloying hint of artificial cinnamon.

But I couldn't enjoy it.

Ever since Sparks and the Wellies mentioned strange characters, I couldn't stop scanning the faces around me. Every person I passed—tourist, local, or performer—got an extra second or two of scrutiny. Were their eyes too bright? Their posture too fluid? Were those footsteps too silent on the gravel?

I was looking for cracks. And the worst part was, I was starting to see them.

"That mime juggling fire over there?" I whispered.

"Left-handed, barefoot, and not blinking nearly enough," Vex murmured from my shoulder. "Definitely not local."

A little girl giggled beside her mother near the bakery cart, her face painted with silver spirals. The symbols weren't from any festival booth I recognized—they were old. Eerily familiar to Dweller script.

"That looks suspiciously like it's from the eastern archives," I said under my breath.

"Someone's teaching." Vex's tail swished once. "Or showing off. Neither is good."

We reached the fountain in the town square. The area was packed again with festivalgoers heading to and from the forest clearing. Some people sipped drinks like sparkling maple lemonade, strawberry basil spritzers, elderflower tonics, and iced raspberry hibiscus teas.

Others ate food like cheddar and herb hand pies, fresh asparagus tartlets, wild ramp and potato soup, and buttermilk squash mac and cheese. Several took selfies, sampled local honey, lined up at the DIY maple taffy booth, and sampled Vermont hard cider and craft beer flights.

It all looked festive.

It all felt wrong.

I spotted Chief Thorn standing stiffly near the bookstore, a cup of steaming coffee in one hand and a small notebook in the other. His dark sport coat and perpetually unimpressed expression gave him the air of a brooding novel detective—if the detective had been forced to chaperone a circus.

He saw me before I waved and slipped his notebook in his coat pocket. "If you're here to sell me a charm, I'll pass," he said dryly as I approached.

"Sorry, fresh out of duck feet and glitter dust."

His lips twitched. Almost a smile. Progress.

Vex leaped from my shoulder and perched on the nearby bench, yawning theatrically.

"You look like you've had the kind of night that ends in a bar fight and a county-wide blackout," he added.

"You're not far off." I sighed.

He raised an eyebrow. "Anything I should know about?"

I glanced around.

A man with unnaturally smooth movements handed out candy with a grin too symmetrical. A teenage girl near the antique shop brushed a hand over the iron railing and muttered something under her breath that I could swear made the metal vibrate.

I shook my head to clear it, probably imagining things.

"Have you noticed any suspicious characters?" I asked. "People who don't seem like they belong?"

His brow furrowed. "Tourists never look like they belong, but yeah...I've noticed a few. Mostly people playing too deep into the folklore. Wearing capes. Quoting old town legends like they're scripture."

"Samuel used to do that too," I admitted.

Holden's jaw tightened. "This whole festival—it's like lighting a match in a dry field. I get that it brings in money, but it brings out the worst in some people. It makes them believe in nonsense. That's what happened to Samuel. He got in too deep. Started chasing fairy stories instead of facing reality, and someone took advantage of that."

I forced a nod, careful to hide my thoughts. "The festival does attract the dreamers, but it also keeps the town alive. We depend on it for our livelihood."

He gave me a look. "Yeah, well. Livelihood or not, someone's dead. All we have are costumed fanatics and people who think they saw actual Dwellers in the town library."

Footsteps scuffed behind us. A vendor pushed a cart of blinking toys that blinked in rhythm—not to any music playing, but to something older. Rhythmic energy patterns. Leylines. As the cart passed, one toy popped. A low electric whine followed, and the lights in the coffee shop behind us flickered wildly before exploding into a shower of sparks.

A collective gasp rose from the crowd.

Thorn instinctively stepped in front of me, his hand on his belt and eyes scanning the area. "Power surge?" he muttered.

"Probably," I lied. "Most likely old wiring mixed with new festival tech." I pulled out my cell phone and text Eli to let him know.

Holden watched the startled barista sweep up glass, and then replied, "Yeah. Or maybe this town is just cursed."

"Maybe." I shrugged, not quite looking at him.

He took a long sip of his drink, then lowered his voice. "My uncle was stationed near the Montpelier site long before I was born. He used to say there were places where the world felt too thin, like something was pressing against it from the other side. I thought he was just crazy until I got stationed here. I have to admit I've seen things I can't explain."

My eyes widened. "You have?"

His gaze met mine, steady and strong. "But I don't believe in monsters, Lyra. The real monsters are people like the ones who killed my father to get back at me. They are flesh and blood. That's what scares me. People who do evil and call it justice."

"I'm so sorry," I said quietly. The vulnerability in his voice caught me off guard. I'd never heard him speak like this. Thorn was duty and logic and steel, but now? Now he was raw. I reached out and squeezed his hand before I realized what I was doing.

He looked at our joined hands but didn't let go. "I'm going to find out what happened to Samuel," he continued, his gaze meeting mine. "And if anyone's using this festival or these stories to hurt people...I'll shut them down, with or without glitter dust."

I gave him a faint smile and slowly pulled my hand away. "Good. Because if one more person pretends to levitate a cupcake, I may retire early."

Thorn barked a short laugh. "Now that I'd pay to see." He

gave Vex a passing glance. "You know, for a cat, he always looks like he's up to something."

"He usually is," I said quickly, reaching to scratch behind his ears.

Vex purred without comment, for once.

Behind us, a breeze from out of nowhere stirred the festival banners. In the shadows near the alley, I thought I saw a flicker of green—like a flash leaped and vanished into the mist. Then I saw a hot air balloon high in the sky. Sparks was still nearby, and so were others, apparently.

It was time I went home.

Eight

UNDER THE COVER of darkness that evening, I cloaked myself and then transported through the portal. Even after all this time, the transition still made my breath catch.

Vex walked beside me, his tail flicking in elegant irritation, fur in his Whispen form slightly raised with tension and movement. He'd insisted on coming this time, but he didn't speak. He didn't need to. I could feel the magic in his paws react to the shifting currents in the air like static before a storm.

My robes whispered around my legs as I moved. I'd shed my earthly clothes for the occasion, dressing in ceremonial garb to honor both halves of my blood. I once again wore a seal made on my own. Leaves stitched in silver thread caught my eye and I thought for a moment about Dweller light and how it played with the stone glittered in green and brown, a nod to human grit.

A symbol of survival, balance, and something different like me.

As the crystal doors ahead shimmered open, the scent of old magic swept over me, cool and sharp like the air before a snowstorm, even though Elarion didn't have seasons. The temperature remained eternally comfortable year-round.

The *Council Chamber* lay ahead, vast and hollow like the inside of a bell carved from moonstone. Twelve elders sat in tiered arcs, each in robes dyed the hues of their roles—starlight silver, ember red, ocean teal, shadow obsidian, and more. Their faces were solemn, ageless, and lit by the glow of hovering memory orbs that rotated above them like slow sentient moons.

And in the center seat of power, elevated above them all, sat Elder Vaerion. He was the Chief Elder of Elarion and Calderis's father.

He looked as if he were forged from pressure: his face all sharp lines and quiet judgment, his silver hair braided with twilight blue thread. His robes shimmered with his seal, a crest of an ancient whirlpool encircling a starburst, woven into his chest in threads that shimmered with old authority. The air around him carried a weight, like the deep silence at the bottom of a lake.

Beside him, leaning against the silver dais like a statue given breath, was his son Calderis, Chief of the Enforcers.

He moved once again like the water—elegant, tall, and dangerous. His cobalt-trimmed robes whispered against the crystal floor, and the sunstone in his crest caught the overhead light. His hair, silver as starlight, flowed in waves down his back, gleaming with each subtle movement. His eyes—blue-gray today, restless and turbulent—locked with mine.

He said nothing.

Neither did I.

"Lyra Wells," Vaerion said at last, his voice low and resonant. "You bring disturbance across the veil."

I stepped forward, my breath steady despite the pulse thudding in my throat. "I bring truth. The disturbance was already here."

"Speak it," Calderis said.

"Samuel Greer is dead."

Gasps and murmurs rose. The floating lights above flickered in response, dimming as if in shock.

"I heard rumors, but I didn't want to believe they were true.

He made a forbidden wish with a stolen wish token," Orielle, Keeper of Lost Voices, said, her voice like wind through reeds.

"And that's why I'm here," I said. "His death wasn't natural. There were no wounds and no illness. He simply...stopped living. And now the well is unbalanced. I've felt it. The veil is leaking, the water levels falling, and Dwellers have crossed through."

"Impossible," scoffed Calderis's comrade, Drelian, his deep green robe crackling with defensive enchantments. He sat beside Calderis.

I held his gaze. "Tell that to the two I passed at the festival. The human world is waking up. If the well doesn't choose a recipient to grant their wish before the final night of WishFest is over, the treaty will collapse."

"The wish cycle must complete," Maelin, Flame Keeper of the Echo Caverns, murmured, her fire-colored hair flickering with ember-light. "Or war will resume and all will burn."

"I've come to ask for your guidance. How do we complete the wish cycle?"

Seris, Keeper of Forbidden Love, spoke gently. "We don't. The well does. As you know, after the humans wish, the well will choose a recipient by the last night of WishFest. But Samuel's unauthorized wish still lingers in the well, clogging it. Justice must be served before the wish can be cleared and a recipient chosen. That's the only way to complete the cycle."

"It is so," said Selvi, the Ice Seer. She was capable of freezing time for a few seconds and seeing fractured visions of possible futures in the reflections. "As I told the Council, I've seen the devastating outcome of what will become of Elarion if Samuel's wish isn't cleared in time and a recipient chosen."

"Then it's agreed," Calderis said quietly. "Lyra can investigate and find who broke the cycle."

Vaerion's nostrils flared. "You propose we allow a half-blood to question our own?"

I bit my tongue and held my silence.

Calderis kept his eyes locked on his father. "I propose we let the one person who bridges both worlds fix the damage before we all pay the price."

I looked to Vaerion. "I will question both humans and Dwellers. I already have some names."

"List them," he said coldly.

"Evelyn Poe, Marin Holloway, and a few possible others I'm looking into," I said. "Each with motive, and each of them have secrets."

"And among us?" Vaerion asked.

I hesitated, then answered, "Sparks, maybe. I saw him in Wishville. He slipped through after Samuel's unauthorized wish cracked the veil." And Weylan the hot air balloon operator if my suspicions were correct. He had blond flowy hair, bright green eyes, was tall, and gave off suspicious vibes. "Sparks could have had contact with Samuel," I continued. "I'm not sure of any others yet, but I've heard some in this realm might have had reason to want to silence him."

"You accuse your own kind," Maelin said, her gaze heating.

"I accuse no one yet," I replied calmly, "but as you all love to point out, I'm part human. I'm the only impartial one belonging to both worlds." They only accepted me as one of their own when it was convenient for them. "The truth is buried beneath too many lies, and we're nearly out of time."

"It's agreed then," Calderis said, stepping closer. "You'll have access to memory crystals, the archives, and whatever else you need. But be careful where you tread, Lyra."

I nodded. "The treaty's hanging by a thread. Only one wish left, one chance to restore the balance, and one chance to save both realms. Got it."

Vaerion finally spoke again. "You have until the sun's rise after the last night of WishFest. After that—"

"The treaty is broken and the veil is lifted," I finished for him, "opening both worlds to war." No pressure.

~

I had just passed the boundary stones when I heard the footsteps behind me—steady, deliberate, boots that whispered instead of stomped.

"I thought you were going to let me go without saying anything to me," I said without turning.

Calderis's voice came from just behind me, low and measured. "I didn't want to distract you."

I stopped beneath a stone arch woven with flowering vines that glowed faintly in the dim light. The petals opened and closed in slow, breathing pulses, responding to our proximity. Everything in Elarion had a pulse.

He had no clue his mere presence distracted me. "You watched as if I were a possible threat." I turned toward him, folding my arms. "Do you believe I am?"

His gaze met mine without hesitation. "No, but I'm not the only one who watches."

He was close now, and I could smell cool rain, crystalline minerals, and sacred woods. His sunstone crest gleamed like liquid fire over his heart, but his expression wasn't fire. It was more like stone—solid and unreadable, but worn smooth in places like something had eroded it over time.

"You did well in there," he said quietly, glancing back toward the *Council Chamber*. "Better than most full-blooded Dwellers would have."

"High praise," I said, half-smiling, "from the enforcer-in-training who nearly arrested me when we were sixteen."

He huffed—something not quite a laugh but not disagreement either. "You were caught stealing an echo blossom from the *Crystal Hollow*. That's a crime."

"It was already dead," I said. "I was trying to keep it from fading."

We fell into step, walking through a narrow pathway that curved around the outer ring of the city. Above us, the biolumi-nescent canopy of the Dreamroot Trees wove together, their branches forming an intricate, moving lace that danced in the breeze. Beneath our feet, the walkway glowed faintly—an embedded trail of light guiding our path like veins through marble.

"I meant to ask," I said, after a while. "Why did you support me in there? You didn't have to."

He didn't answer right away. We passed through a courtyard filled with pools, the water as still as glass. Soft orbs drifted above the surface, casting amber ripples on the high-vaulted ceiling.

"My father wants me to become an Elder," he said finally. "He's expected it since the moment I learned to speak. Legacy, he calls it. Heir to the chief position."

I looked over at him. "You're the oldest son."

He nodded once. "But I've never wanted it. I was never good at stillness or debating. I wanted motion and justice. I joined the Enforcers the day I came of age, even though it nearly broke us."

"Nearly?"

His jaw hardened. "My mother and sister understood. My father saw it as rebellion. A waste."

"You're not a waste," I said before I could stop myself.

He glanced at me then, something unspoken flickering behind his eyes. "Tell that to a man who only sees worth in silence and ceremony."

We walked quietly for a moment more. Somewhere far above a cavern hawk cried out, its wings slicing through shafts of amber light like a ghost against the ceiling.

"I'm closer with my mother," he said suddenly, adding, "and my youngest sister. They still send me river stones carved with old blessings." The corners of his lips tipped up slightly. "I keep them in my quarters."

"That sounds...peaceful." He was lucky to still have Elanith and Lumira with him. I'd give anything for one more day with my mother.

He nodded. "They remind me why I protect this place."

I slowed near a wall of memory crystals—each one suspended in a ripple of water, glowing faintly with captured voices, dreams, and moments long past. How had Samuel gotten ahold of one...or who had given it to him?

"You know this place better than anyone," I said. "You feel the shifts before the council even acknowledges them. Do you feel it now?"

"Yes." He nodded. "Something's wrong. It's not just Samuel's death. It's what he stirred. What he uncovered."

I touched one of the crystals. It glowed faintly under my fingers. "He was asking the right questions."

Calderis studied the crystals, his expression unreadable. "If you want a place to start...my source says talk to Reed Callahan again. The clockmaker."

My brows rose. "You think Reed's involved?"

"I don't know, but I've seen his name crop up in more than one recent anomaly report. Unstable energy spikes. Temperature fluctuations near the surface gate. Reed's workshop isn't far from that."

I tilted my head. "Did you tell the Council that?"

"No." He shook his head. "Vaerion would say it's speculation, and speculation isn't legacy-worthy."

I smiled despite myself. "And here you are, risking your perfect record."

"I've never cared about records," he said, facing me again. "I care about keeping both our worlds from collapsing, and I trust your judgment."

Something passed between us then—something old and familiar and complicated. A memory of the first time he helped me out of the veil when I fell through as a child. The way he watched me like I was both a danger and a miracle.

"I'll look into Reed," I said softly. "Thank you."

We stood in the hush of the crystal wall for a moment longer. A faint tremor passed through the stones under our feet, barely noticeable but real.

Calderis turned sharply. "Did you feel that?"

I nodded slowly. "Another crack?"

"Or something waking up. Can you temporarily stabilize the cracks in the well?"

"I can try, but until the unauthorized wish is cleared, I fear more cracks will form."

He nodded once.

The light overhead dimmed slightly, and for a moment the city's usual serenity felt...tense. On edge, as if someone were watching.

"I should go," I said, my voice hushed now.

Calderis's hand brushed mine—a soft touch that anchored me. "Be careful, Lyra."

I turned slightly, but he wasn't finished.

His gaze shifted, more guarded now. "Humans aren't the only danger. Elarion has become divided."

"How so?" I asked, my voice barely a whisper.

"A rebellion is forming with Dwellers like Thayn leading the resistance." His mouth formed a flat line. "He's been stirring unrest among the outer caverns, preaching that the surface treaty is a lie." He paused a beat. "That the veil's weakness is an opportunity."

I frowned. "I thought he went into self-contemplation after the winter solstice."

Calderis's mouth twisted into a bitter smile. "That's what his family says, but I'm not so sure." His gaze met mine. "He hasn't been seen in a while."

My breath quickened. "Do you think he crossed through?"

"I'm not sure," Calderis said, his voice like stone. "Just be careful up there."

The Dreamroot canopy above us flickered again, and silver shadows danced across Calderis's cheekbones. I caught a glimpse of something softer there. Worry...or something else.

"I'll start with Reed," I said, my voice steady with resolve, "and I'll be careful. I promise."

His gaze lingered on me like he wanted to say something else

—something not about suspects or treaties or ancestral crests. But instead, he said, "Lyra? If you go after Reed...don't go alone."

"I won't," I lied and then stepped into the archway, Vex materializing at my heels, his tail held high.

Behind me, the city of Elarion glistened, beautiful and silent and brimming with secrets. And somewhere within that silence, truth waited—twisted with lies woven through crystal and tangled in roots deeper than I'd ever dared to dig. But I would because I had no choice. Whether I liked it or not...

I was the only hope for both our worlds.

THE GEARS on *Callahan's Creations & Clocks* clanked twice before the lock gave way and the door creaked open with a sound like a drawn-out sigh—a mechanical groan that echoed into the early morning light. I stepped into Reed's workshop, and the scent hit me first: metal filings, scorched wood, and something sharp beneath it all like static electricity in the air before a lightning strike.

Clock faces in every size lined the far wall, their ticking out of sync. Cogs, wires, and delicate gears lay in trays on long oak workbenches, each labeled in Reed's sharp, spidery handwriting. The whole place hummed with the intensity of focus, the kind born from years of solitude and obsession.

I could feel it in the air—a buzz in my fingertips, a prickling behind my eyes—like time itself was holding its breath.

Vex, as always, slinked ahead of me as if he owned the place. His tail flicked at a crooked grandfather clock that ticked backward, then stopped entirely with a sullen thunk.

"Reed?" I called, my voice a little louder than it needed to be. "Got a minute?"

He emerged from behind a curtain of copper chain links, wiping his soot-streaked hands on a dark apron that looked like it had weathered a dozen small explosions. His thick glasses magnified his hazel eyes until he looked like clockwork himself. Stray hairs curled behind his ears, and one of his sleeves was singed at the cuff.

"If you're here to ask about my missing prototype, Lyra, I still haven't found it," he said, rubbing his temples. His voice was frayed at the edges like an old recording.

"I didn't know you had a missing prototype. That's not why I'm here," I lied smoothly.

He narrowed his eyes. "Then why are you here?"

"Because Samuel Greer's death is a mystery." I stepped closer, lowering my voice as the ticking around us grew louder. "Your workshop is just beyond the well, and suspicious activity involving fluctuating temperatures was reported by an anonymous source." I couldn't tell him Calderis is the one who told me. "Since I'm chair of WishFest, part of my job is making sure the festival is safe."

Reed stiffened. His hand went to a dial on his wrist—a tiny, spinning compass-like device. "There was a cold spell that night, remember? Of course, the temperature was going to fluctuate after that."

"Ah, but you said Samuel was snooping around your shop looking for a temperature tracking mechanism, and now your prototype is missing."

Reed's shoulders tensed. "I didn't kill him. I told you, he broke in. He was obsessed with tracking any anomalies surrounding the well. Said he wanted to expose the truth about the well. I think he stole my unfinished mechanism. I'm an inventor, not a magician. I developed a prototype that didn't just measure temperature fluctuations but caused them as well. It was unstable. Not ready. It could've messed with his perception." Reed looked into my eyes with genuine concern. "Samuel might have accidentally caused his own death."

I crossed my arms. "Why didn't you report it missing?"

"Would you, if it meant the town council might ban your work altogether? They already think I'm as crazy as Samuel, and look what happened to him."

"Are you?" I watched him closely. He had *mad scientist* written all over him. "Your inventions are a little unorthodox, and you do become a bit obsessed about them."

Reed huffed, pushing up his glasses. "I build tools for understanding, detecting, and observing what others pretend don't exist. It's harmless. I'm not hurting anyone."

"Yet Samuel is dead."

"Not by my hand, I swear."

I glanced at the far wall. A chalkboard had the words "CALIBRATION FAILURE" scrawled across the top, and beneath it, a jagged line graph dipped erratically. Dates were scribbled in the margin. The last one was the night Samuel died.

The night of the cold snap.

"Reed," I said carefully. "If you're lying to me, and someone else dies because of it..."

"I'm not," he snapped, then immediately deflated. "I'm not. But if Samuel or someone else used my invention incorrectly, they might have inadvertently caused the cold snap. What's to stop them from doing so again...or worse?"

"You'd better hope they don't." I turned toward the door. The scent of oil and solder still clung to the back of my throat.

"Wait," he called. "If you're serious about looking into this...check out Hollow Glen. Someone tried to test something there last week, and now there's a large crater. You'll see the pattern burned into the grass."

I didn't answer. Vex and I slipped outside. The workshop door groaned shut behind us, its hinges squealing like a warning.

"Lyra Wells, what are you up to now?" a deep voice said from behind me.

I flinched.

Chief Holden Thorn stood near the edge of the path, his arms crossed and expression unreadable behind his aviator sunglasses. He looked carved from granite, all grim lines and tension.

"I'm not up to anything," I said, trying to keep my voice level. "Just checking in with one of the locals."

"Then why do you look suspicious?"

I dropped my hands to my spandex-clad hips. "According to you, I am the most suspicious person of interest when there are other suspects to look into."

He stepped closer. I could smell cedar and a hint of something more—his aftershave, probably, but it made my stomach twist unexpectedly. "That's *my* job, Lyra. You're not a cop. You're the festival liaison. Keep the tourists happy and stick to your role."

"People text me if I'm needed, but I can't keep WishFest running smoothly if people are scared there's a murderer on the loose."

His eyes narrowed, and his jaw flexed. "Trust that I'm doing my job."

"Are you?" I challenged. "Have you even questioned Evelyn Poe? She said she and Samuel matched on some dating app. She was practically stalking him because he wouldn't go out with her. What about Marin Holloway? She'd been hounding him for a story—pushed so hard she probably knew more about his movements than anyone."

Holden scowled. "I'm focusing on Rowan Baxter."

I blinked. "Rowan?"

"Samuel accused him of stealing annotated folklore maps. They had a blowout at the Historical Society three days before his death. Witnesses heard it. Rowan's gloves had moss that matched the well's base."

I'd missed that meeting but had heard about the argument. "And his alibi?"

"Says he was home cataloguing artifacts alone."

Vex growled low in his throat, a sound that vibrated through my boots.

"Look," I said, trying to soften my voice. "I'm not trying to take your badge. But if we both want answers, maybe we don't work against each other?"

Thorn's expression flickered. For a moment, he looked less like the town's protector and more like a man trying very hard to hold something together. "Then stop sneaking around and interfering with my case," he muttered. "You think you can do that?"

I nodded, my heartbeat quickening, but I didn't verbally agree to anything.

He hesitated, studying me as if he didn't believe me, then he nodded once. "Good. Now, go home, and keep your nose out of trouble please."

I didn't reply. Just gave him a wave and turned toward town, the spring breeze cool against my flushed cheeks. Because if Reed was right, and someone had used his unstable prototype...then we weren't just dealing with the unfortunate death of one man.

Humans had no idea what the effects of their actions could be.

I wanted to tell Holden what I had discovered, but he would think I was the one who had gone crazy, even if I told him I didn't believe it. I needed to find that device before disaster happened. A device that could drastically change temperatures could lead to all sorts of natural disasters.

What happened above the well could also change life below the well...permanently.

The late afternoon sun filtered through the canopy of trees, dappling the forest floor in flickering designs as I made my way toward Hollow Glen. The trees grew denser the farther I walked, branches weaving together overhead like ancient fingers locking secrets between them. The air was cooler here, laced with the scent of pine needles and damp earth.

I inhaled deeply, grounding myself in that wild, primal stillness.

I had updated Calderis with my Elarion crystal phone before heading to the glen. And I had kept my promise. I hadn't talked to Reed alone and I wasn't alone now. Vex padded beside me, utterly silent except for the occasional rustle of underbrush beneath his paws. His black fur blended seamlessly into the gathering shadows, but his tail twitched with wary curiosity. His ears flicked constantly, attuned to sounds the human half of my senses couldn't catch.

The trail had long since stopped being a trail—just a faint suggestion of passage now, a barely-there swath where grass lay flattened and leaves had been disturbed. My boots sank slightly into the soft loam as I climbed a shallow ridge, one hand brushing the rough bark of a birch trunk for balance.

Seismic Sense enabled me to feel vibrations through the earth to guide the way. When I reached the crest, I saw it.

The crater.

It was worse than I'd imagined and far bigger.

How had we not heard or seen anything? A jagged wound in the earth, as if some celestial hand had pressed a burning brand into the ground and then torn it away. The rim was ringed in blackened grass, curled and brittle like lace left too close to a flame. Ash clung to every surface, and a faint heat still shimmered in the air above it.

I stepped closer, my scuffed boots brushing against charred weeds. Wind tugged at my loose hair. I swept it into a ponytail, not having to worry about my birthmark here. My dryfit shirt, no longer dry, clung to my back damp from sweat. I knelt carefully at the edge, brushing a piece of dirt from my cheek with fingers that trembled more than I liked. My gaze fell on the center of the crater —and my breath caught.

There it was. Just as Reed had described.

A pattern.

Not random scorch marks, not the chaos of wildfire or lightning, this was crafted. Designed. Spirals, intersecting lines, and curled etchings that formed a perfect burn signature—like a sigil branded into the earth by some unseen force.

I reached out, hesitant, and pressed my fingertips to one of the lines. It was still warm.

Too warm for the time of day. Too warm for this to be a relic from hours ago. This was recent. Fresh.

A wave of nausea crept up from my stomach and settled behind my ribs.

The scorched vines that ringed the far edge were too familiar. They curled in the same distinctive way as the one we'd found near the well after Samuel's death—twisted and blackened with a strange, oily sheen. I stared at them, frozen, until Calderis's voice echoed unbidden in my mind, telling of the fracture Thayn had caused in Elarion.

Could this be a rebel Dweller, maybe?

The thought chilled me more than the breeze now stirring the trees around me.

Dweller rebels believed the treaty was a mistake. They claimed the surface world had poisoned *their kind* and should be purged. They wanted to reclaim the land that had once belonged to the Dwellers...even if it meant wiping out humanity to do it.

What if one of them had found Samuel that night?

What if Samuel really had stolen the prototype—the temperature device Reed swore was still in testing? What if a rebel had taken it...used it? Could that have triggered the unnatural cold snap, freezing Samuel before he could even cry out?

The rebels might not understand that manipulating the surface world could ripple across dimensions. Altering Wishville's climate might destabilize Elarion itself. Then again...maybe they *did* understand.

Maybe they just didn't care.

I took a step into the crater to examine a second cluster of symbols. The world tilted, dropped out from beneath me, and I screamed. My boots slipped on loose gravel as I tumbled forward, hitting the slope hard. Pain bloomed instantly in my knees, sharp and throbbing, and my palms scraped raw against jagged stone.

I cursed under my breath, my adrenaline spiking as I pushed up on bleeding hands only to slide again. Dirt crumbled under me in thick clumps, and the air was suddenly sharp with the copper tang of blood and the sting of fear.

"Vex!" I shouted, my voice ragged.

I could hear him yowling somewhere above me, a mournful, urgent cry. I saw movement. He was pacing along the rim, his shadow flickering as he circled, his tail lashing. I struggled upright again, one boot slipping as I tried to gain footing. The crater was steep and deeper than I'd realized from above.

I was stuck.

Cold seeped into my skin, the kind that went bone-deep—unnatural and biting. Dusk had arrived faster than I'd expected, blanketing the forest. And then I heard them.

Wolves.

A low, keening howl rose from somewhere to my left, followed by another...closer. My heart thundered in my chest. The forest had gone silent. Too silent. No rustle of birds, no chirp of crickets, just that eerie hush—the kind that made you feel like prey. Then I heard a crunch like footsteps. Slow, measured, deliberate...

Not animal.

My throat tightened. I twisted, trying to locate the source, but the shadows twisted everything, and everything looked like a threat.

"Who's there?" I called, my voice cracking.

Nothing.

Then, with a sudden gust that sent leaves spinning in a frenzy, something passed overhead. A deep, steady *whoosh-whoosh* of air. I looked up and gasped.

A hot air balloon.

A patchwork canopy of deep red and sunset orange hovered above the trees like a dream—or a hallucination. The basket dipped low, and a rope ladder unfurled down the side, swaying gently.

"Hold on!" a voice called, warm and unmistakable.

Weylan.

Relief swelled in my chest, tangled with suspicion.

I wasn't sure if he was friend or foe, but right now, he seemed like the lesser of all evils in the shadows. I didn't hesitate. I grabbed the ladder, the coarse rope burning against my raw palms, and began to climb. Each step sent fire shooting through my scraped knees, but I didn't stop.

When I reached the basket, Weylan leaned over and gripped my wrists, hauling me inside with a grunt. I collapsed to the floor, panting.

"You alright?" he asked, crouching beside me, his usual easy expression shaded with concern.

"Define alright," I muttered, forcing a weak laugh. "How did you find me?"

He hesitated, then smiled crooked. "I felt a shift in the air."

I blinked, my heart skipping a beat. "What does *that* mean?"

As the balloon rose gently above the treetops, Weylan's expression sobered. He looked out at the forest as if seeing something far beyond it. "I'm not just a balloon tour guide," he said quietly. "I'm a messenger. I travel short distances between realms. My body rides the wind."

The pieces clicked. "I knew it," I whispered. "You're a Dweller."

As part human, Skycall allowed me to influence wind gusts and even the direction birds flew in. But my powers were nothing compared to Weylan's. As a Dweller, Breeze Weaver allowed him to weave gentle breezes, controlling air currents and travel winds to steer his balloon.

He nodded. "Calderis stationed me here to observe. To protect, if needed."

I tamped down my frustration that Calderis didn't trust me to do my job alone, and then arched a brow as Weylan's words sank in. "Protect? You let me fall into a crater."

He grinned. "I didn't say I was *good* at it."

I snorted, a startled laugh escaping me, and the tension in my chest eased slightly.

His voice dropped again. "You were right to come check out

the crater, but you have to be more careful. After your meeting with Calderis, he gave me a heads up to be on the lookout and keep an eye on you. Your Harmony Pulse has worn off. He is afraid there are more Dwellers who might have slipped through the crack. They are extremists and unstable."

I stared down at the darkening forest. "Yeah," I whispered. "I'm starting to get that."

Then panic clutched my chest. "Vex! Where is he?" He'd been trying to reach me right up until Weylan showed up, then he grew quiet.

Weylan sighed. "Gone. He took one look at me and bolted."

I blew out a breath in relief. "That's just his way. He doesn't like anyone."

"Charming creature."

I smiled faintly, but the flickering lights of Wishville loomed closer, a silent reminder that darkness was coming.

CHAPTER

Ten

IF I EVER DOUBTED THAT my life had spiraled out of control, the sight of Chief Holden Thorn standing with arms crossed, waiting for me to disembark from a hot air balloon in the middle of the town square, pretty much sealed it. Weylan had gotten carried away, causing the wind to blow us off course. I tried to redirect the wind gusts, but we missed the landing pad on the festival grounds up the hill. Weylan had quickly pulled the rope, opening a vent at the top of the balloon, allowing the hot air to escape and the balloon to lower to the ground.

Sometimes the human way was safer than magic gone awry.

Townsfolks and outsiders alike gave us a wide berth.

The balloon's shadow loomed large over the cobblestones, its velvet red and sunset fabric still billowing gently in the fading light. The wicker basket creaked as I climbed awkwardly down the rope ladder, my boots slipping once against the rungs. A gust of wind chose that moment to whip my ponytail into my mouth, and I landed on the grass like a clumsy Mary Poppins who had clearly flunked finishing school.

I shot Weylan a frown and he shrugged, looking guilty as I stood, brushing dirt off my torn, damp spandex pants. "Thanks,

Weylan," I said, giving him a look that said I would get even with him.

Weylan waved to me and then saluted Holden as he opened a valve to a large burner to release propane gas. The gas ignited, creating a massive flame that heated the air inside the balloon. The giant colorful sphere began to lift off the ground, and within minutes, he was gone.

Holden didn't flinch. He stood statue-still, the crisp collar on his button-down shirt unwrinkled beneath his sport coat. His jaw was set in that way he had when he was fighting the urge to lecture, and his eyes—those sharp, storm-gray eyes—dropped immediately to my hands and knees.

"That must be some tour. Did the balloon land in a briar patch?" he asked dryly, his voice cool and clipped.

I glanced down. Blood and ash streaked my palms. The once-smooth skin of my knees was now scraped raw and peppered with tiny gravel bits clinging stubbornly to torn leggings. I crossed my boots at the ankles self-consciously.

"Technically...I fell *before* the balloon showed up," I muttered.

"Ah. So, the briar patch came first. That clears things right up." He didn't smile. His expression was pure Holden: unimpressed, deeply skeptical, and absolutely dying to cuff someone for poor judgment.

I tried brushing dirt off my shirt, but all I did was smear charcoal-gray smudges on my sleeves, creating an abstract art piece in woodland grime. The scent of smoke still clung to my clothes from the crater—sharp, burnt earth, and something faintly metallic.

"I wasn't trying to cause a scene," I said.

"Yet here you are," he replied, taking a step closer. "Filthy, limping, and arriving by balloon like the grand finale of a circus act." His sigh was long and deep. "What were you doing near Hollow Glen?"

"How did you—"

"Nothing gets by me, Lyra." His eyes narrowed. "You should know that by now."

His tone wasn't angry, but there was tension humming beneath the words. He didn't just sound irritated...he sounded scared. That low, tight kind of fear that simmered behind control. I'd seen it before on the night Samuel died.

The night Holden thought he might lose someone else.

"I was just walking," I lied, wincing at how weak it sounded. "Okay, more like *investigating* mysterious things. I didn't think it would turn into an adventure."

Holden's jaw tightened. "You didn't think. That part tracks."

"I found a crater, Holden."

His eyes snapped to mine, sharp and intense. "A what?"

"A crater in the woods, burned around the edges like something fell or exploded. And in the center, there was this pattern of scorched lines in a spiral. It didn't look natural. I tried to get a closer look, but the edge crumbled, and I fell in. I couldn't climb out. I yelled, but no one was around. Weylan just happened to be passing overhead."

"How convenient," Holden said flatly.

"He was on a practice run for his tour and saw me, thank goodness. He dropped the ladder and pulled me up then insisted on flying me back like some airborne Uber."

Holden went quiet.

The sounds of the festival floated down from the clearing: laughter and mandolin music, the sizzle of something being fried at a food stall, and the low murmur of townsfolk milling about. The square was just as busy. Strings of fairy lights draped from lamppost to lamppost and on storefronts, casting a warm glow over the cobblestone streets as dusk turned to dark.

But Holden didn't take his eyes off me.

"You could've gotten stuck out there all night," he said eventually. "In a crater, alone, and bleeding with wolves nearby."

"I heard them howling," I admitted, shivering at the memory.

"I didn't wait around to introduce myself." A nervous chuckle slipped out.

"You think this is funny?"

"No." My voice softened. "I think it's dangerous. That's *why* I went. I had to see if what Reed said was true."

Holden's face darkened. "Reed?"

"Reed Callahan, the inventor and clockmaker. He told Samuel about a prototype—a device that might affect temperature. He said it wasn't finished, but what if Samuel took it? What if it malfunctioned?"

Holden looked like he wanted to argue, but he didn't. He rubbed a hand down his face, scrubbing the weariness from his features.

Before he could respond, a new voice floated in from the left.

"Oh, *there* you are, dearie," Belle called, sashaying down the street like it was a runway.

She wore a sweeping green cloak over a sparkling tulle skirt and carried a basket brimming with notes of lord-only-knew-what ready for her messenger pigeons. Her silver hair gleamed under the lampposts, and her bangles jingled like tiny wind chimes.

She didn't even look at Holden before zeroing in on me. "How was your trip? I told you this festival had a twist coming."

Holden turned his shocked stare on her then back to me. "You told her but not me?"

"I didn't tell her anything," I said, lifting my hands, baffled and slightly alarmed. I knew gossip ran fast in a small town, but this had literally just happened. "I guess nothing gets by her, either."

Belle smiled like the cat who had predicted the canary's demise. "I said the winds were shifting," she announced. "And what are winds if not the breath of fate?"

Holden looked like he was mentally calculating how many laws she was currently violating just by speaking in metaphors. "She fell into a crater by her own carelessness." He gestured at me. "It had nothing to do with fate."

"Oh right. Magic, then," Belle said breezily. "The energy's been all wrong since that poor man died. I told Tilly the trees were humming."

"She did," came Tilly's voice as she joined us, a whiff of lavender wafting from her gray braid. "I thought it was indigestion but turns out it was the old oak near the courthouse. They have their own language, you know."

"I'll be sure to alert the tree patrol," Holden grumbled.

"Why, that's a grand idea." Tilly clapped her hands. "Thank you, Chief." She waddled off.

Belle gave him a wink and sashayed after Tilly.

Holden turned back to me, his shoulders stiff. "Don't let them distract you. You could've been seriously hurt. You need to stop doing this alone."

"I know," I said. "I'm done being reckless, but I can't ignore these clues. This murder needs to be solved so the festival can continue without a cloud hanging over the festivities."

Holden exhaled slowly. "Since you clearly won't stay out of my investigation, and you do seem to know more about the well and festival than anyone, would you like to help me as a consultant?"

It's about time, I wanted to say, but settled for, "Yes."

He hesitated. "Okay...on one condition."

I tilted my head. "Name it."

"You don't lie to me anymore. Not about where you're going, who you're talking to, or what dangerous lead you're following next. Deal?"

I grinned. "Deal."

He reached into his coat pocket and handed me a tissue. "You're bleeding."

"Occupational hazard of being nosy."

"I'm going to need a new first aid kit just for you."

Before I could respond, Vex emerged from an alley, his tail swishing like a banner of disdain. He leaped into my arms with practiced flair, kneading my shoulder once before curling up like a spoiled prince.

"Where did he come from?" Holden asked with a raised eyebrow.

"He was with me at the crater, but he doesn't like Weylan, so he found his way back to Wishville on his own." I shrugged.

"You bring the cat on all your adventures?"

"He's my emotional support feline."

Holden barked out a laugh. "He's doing a terrible job."

Vex blinked slowly and licked his paw with absolute indifference, keeping his thoughts to himself for once.

Holden turned toward the precinct. "Come on. We'll patch you up and go over this Reed theory of yours. And Lyra?"

"Yeah?"

"Next time you get the urge to investigate *mysterious things*," he made a set of air quotes with his fingers, "call me first."

"I thought you didn't believe in *mysterious things*." I made a set of air quotes of my own.

"I don't," he paused a beat, his eyes locking onto mine, "but I believe in you."

And that's a start, I thought, my insides warming as I walked beside him.

The police station was quiet, save for the hum of the fluorescent lights and the faint clatter of Holden rummaging through the emergency drawer in his desk. If the sun were still out, I could have healed myself by channeling the warmth and light of the sun using Sunfire Touch. But it was dark, I was tired, and frankly at his mercy.

He pulled out a battered first aid kit the size of a small toolbox and plunked it down in front of me like a man preparing for triage. "Sit," he ordered, pulling off his jacket and rolling up his sleeves then dousing his hands with hand sanitizer.

I obeyed, perching on the edge of the cracked vinyl chair across from his desk, wincing as dried blood tugged against the torn fabric of my leggings.

"Hold still," he muttered, crouching down before me and cutting my leggings to slide them up above my knees.

I resisted the urge to slap my hands on my thighs. His touch was gentle despite the gruffness. The scent of antiseptic mixed with something else—his cologne, maybe—earthy, sharp, like cedar and storms.

"Are you always this prepared?" I asked as he opened a packet of alcohol wipes.

"Yes, but you've made me upgrade my supplies in anticipation of you going rogue. Turns out I wasn't wrong."

"Touché."

"Hold still or I'm taking you out back and getting the hose."

I hissed as he dabbed at a scrape on my knee. "That's a bit dramatic."

He raised a brow. "Says the woman who fell into a questionable crater and escaped via a hot air balloon."

"Point taken."

He bandaged my knees and my palms as if he'd done so many times before, probably from his days in the military, then he leaned back and inspected his work. The air between us charged with energy. He didn't say anything, but I caught the flicker of something—concern, frustration, maybe something else entirely— as he smoothed a corner of the medical tape over a square of gauze on my skin before carefully pulling my leggings back down.

"There," he said, rising. "You won't win any beauty contests, but you'll live."

"Well, that's comforting."

He tossed the wrappers in the bin, then leaned against the desk and crossed his arms. "You eaten?"

"Today?"

He gave me a flat look.

I squirmed. "No."

He pushed off the desk. "Come on. We're going to *The Wishbone.*"

I blinked. "Like...for dinner?"

He didn't answer right away. Just grabbed his jacket and held the door open. "You need to eat."

"Oh. Right. Sure." My voice pitched awkwardly high. "Not a date. Just dinner. Sustenance. Casual food-based survival."

His mouth twitched like he was fighting a smile, but he didn't comment. He just led the way out the door.

The Wishbone Café was dim and cozy, all reclaimed wood and mismatched chairs. The scent of rosemary and garlic wafted from the kitchen. Soft jazz played through the speakers, and clusters of locals filled the booths and barstools, including Eli the handyman, Bart the butcher, and Gus the barber. Warm lighting, comfort food, the clink of mugs and silverware filled the air.

We slid into a corner booth. Holden ordered us two draft beers and the roast chicken special without even asking me. Honestly? I was too tired to argue and too hungry to care.

"So," he said, after our drinks arrived. "Reed Callahan. Tell me everything."

I wrapped my hands around the glass, grateful for the cold against my bandages. "As I said earlier, he's an inventor. Eccentric. A bit of a recluse. He has a clock shop near the well that half the town forgets exists."

"I've seen his shop but haven't met him yet. I've heard he's a little odd," Holden said. "Heard he built a weathervane that predicted a solar eclipse two years late."

"Yeah, well...he's more successful with machines than calendars." I took a sip of ice-cold beer. "He told me he'd been working on a prototype—a device that measures atmospheric fluctuations, particularly temperature anomalies." I watched him closely, wondering how much I could tell him. How much he would believe.

Holden snorted. "You mean weather."

"No. I mean...magic." I met his gaze.

"Now hold on, Lyra..." He raised a hand to cut me off, but I couldn't stop. If Holden and I were going to be an investigative team, he needed to know this information.

"Just hear me out." I paused as his hand slowly returned to the table. "Reed thinks it can *cause* changes, too, and not just record them. A sharp drop in temperature or a freeze, maybe, like what happened the night Samuel died."

Holden leaned back. "You're telling me Reed Callahan made a cold machine?"

"Not *just* cold. Shifts. Pressure, temperature...maybe even perception. He said it wasn't stable. He wasn't ready to show it to anyone, but Samuel was pushing him. And now Samuel's dead...and the prototype's gone."

Holden studied me over the rim of his beer. "You think someone stole it."

"I *know* it's missing. The prototype's gone, his workshop's a mess, and Reed confirmed it himself."

Holden was quiet for a beat. "Let's say I buy this," he said finally. "Not that it works, but that someone stole Reed's mystery machine. Who would want it?"

I exhaled. "That's the problem. Someone with enough knowledge to know what it could do and enough motive to use it."

"To cover a crime," Holden murmured.

"Exactly. What if Samuel found out something he shouldn't have? Maybe he threatened to go public, and someone used the prototype to silence him. To make it look like an accident. A freak cold snap."

"Or good timing, coinciding with the weather." Holden tapped his fingers against his glass. "You really believe that machine killed him? I mean, I suppose it could have used something like liquid nitrogen and then blew up causing the scorch marks." He shrugged. "Anything's possible."

"I think it *could* have killed Samuel for sure."

Holden didn't respond right away. He just stared at the condensation trailing down his glass. "I'm not saying I believe the thing's magical, but...I've seen some pretty strange things lately. And if it was used in any capacity to hurt Samuel, I want to know."

"Thank you," I said softly, relieved he hadn't outright dismissed my theories, and grateful he was a man of his word when he'd said he believed in me.

He looked up. "Don't thank me yet. We're going to make a list. Anyone with access to Reed. Anyone who might've wanted to shut Samuel up."

"I've been thinking about other suspects for a while now." Just like I'd told the Council of Elders, but I'd needed time to form a list. I pulled out my phone and tapped into my notes. "What about Henry McAlister? I thought I saw him in town yesterday."

"Right, that land developer who proposed a modern redevelopment project of the well," Holden added.

"Which the Historical Society said no to, of course," I interjected, "with Samuel being one of the biggest members opposed to the idea."

"That's not surprising, given Samuel lived in the past as an antique dealer," Holden responded.

"The mayor, however, has shown an interest which has given McAlister hope. He even claims she invited him to attend the last zoning meeting. He says he went, gave a speech, and gained support for his project," I said, laden with contempt. "I wouldn't put it past Henry to do something to shut Samuel up so he can push his project through. He's hands-on with his construction crew and knows a lot about machines. He could have used the machine on Samuel or the well."

"That's a bit of a reach, but worth looking into." Holden took a sip of his beer. "Who else do you have?"

"Gavin Rhoades. He's an archaeologist who is obsessed with the legend of the well, Elarion, and Dwellers. He attends WishFest every season and has been trying to find the lost city for years."

"Didn't Gavin and Samuel have a run-in a while back? At least that was in the files the last police chief left for me."

"Yes. Samuel turned him in for digging around the woods without a permit." I slapped my palm on the table as the lightbulb went off in my brain. "What if Gavin stole the machine to get Samuel out of his way, and maybe he created the crater at Hollow Glen? He could be widening his search area?"

"You sure do have some unusual theories and quirky characters in your town, but I suppose it wouldn't hurt to look into him, too."

Our meals arrived—crispy chicken, garlic mashed potatoes, and roasted carrots drizzled in balsamic glaze. I nearly cried at the first bite. Holden pretended not to notice, but I saw his smirk just before I closed my eyes in delight.

"Food this good *has* to be magic," I said around a mouthful of potato.

He grunted. "You're just underfed."

I didn't disagree. "Too much to do. Too little time. Too busy to cook."

We were halfway through our meal when a familiar voice rang out from across the room.

"There she is! Our crater queen!"

I turned just in time to see Dot striding toward us in a polka dot purple shawl and a glittery T-shirt that read *I Predict Mayhem.* She pushed her oversized spectacles further up her nose and blinked her owl eyes at us.

I should have known the news of my crater encounter would have already spread.

She plopped down in the booth beside me, uninvited and unapologetic. "I heard you came out of the sky like Dorothy in Oz. Tell me everything."

"Maybe later. I'm trying to have dinner," I said gently.

"Exactly! Dinner gossip is the *best* gossip. What did the crater smell like? Was it sulfur? Ozone? Cosmic regret? Did you meet the wicked witch?"

Holden gave her a long, slow sigh. "Dot."

"Chief Thorn," she said sweetly. "Still keeping all the fun to yourself?"

I smiled despite myself. "No witch, but it smelled like burned grass and conspiracy."

"Oh, *juicy!*" Dot clapped her hands. "I knew something was going to happen this week. My armpit itched in Morse code on Tuesday."

Holden pinched the bridge of his nose.

Dot pulled a candy from her purse and handed it to me. "Protection sweet," she whispered. "Lemon balm and sea salt. Keep it on your person. It'll protect you from the flying monkeys."

"Thanks, Dot," I said, pocketing it.

She leaned in and stage-whispered, "If you hear disembodied whistling tonight, don't answer. That's how they *mark* you."

"Got it. No whistling." And no idea who *they* were.

With a satisfied nod, she bounced off toward the bar to join Belle and Tilly who were giving Trip an earful. He was hanging on their every word and taking notes.

Holden watched her go and muttered, "If anyone's weaponized that prototype, it's probably them."

"I wouldn't be surprised," I said, "but they mean well."

"They are walking distractions."

"Sometimes distractions lead you to answers."

Holden looked at me for a long beat, then he nodded almost reluctantly. "Let's track our suspects down tomorrow together."

Something fluttered in my chest—fear maybe, or hope, or something far more dangerous. "Okay," I said. "Together."

Right after I informed Calderis of my new suspect list.

CHAPTER
Eleven

THE NEXT MORNING, Wishville looked like it had been tucked beneath a gray wool blanket. Fog hung low in the streets, and a persistent drizzle misted the windows of storefronts, making everything glisten like a watercolor painting left out in the rain. The scent of damp earth and chimney smoke clung to the air, mingling with the faint aroma of honey lavender shortbread wafting from *The Twisted Loaf.*

As promised, I'd updated Calderis. Weylan had already informed him of my crater debacle, which he wasn't happy about. Which was why I'd thought he'd be pleased when I told him I was partnering with Holden to look into the rest of the suspects. Yet his voice had sounded funny. Irritated.

Jealous almost.

I closed my umbrella, shaking off that crazy thought, as I stepped onto the slick stone steps of the *County Clerk's Office*, my boots leaving faint prints on the wet flagstones. Inside, the building had that particular hum of bureaucracy—old fluorescent lights buzzing overhead, the click of outdated keyboards, and the faint whir of a copy machine that sounded one paper jam away from retirement.

The *Zoning Office* was on the second floor, tucked beside a room used exclusively for filing noise complaints and tax grievances. Amanda Carter sat behind her desk, a queen among chaos. Her chair squeaked each time she shifted, and her desk was layered with half-drunk coffee cups and multi-colored highlighters like she was building a shrine to caffeine and mild panic.

"You're here about something weird, aren't you?" she said before I even opened my mouth. She wore a sweater covered in sequined squirrels wielding acorns like swords and held a pencil behind each ear like antennae for municipal gossip.

I smiled. "Define weird."

"I heard you met the great and powerful wizard in the woods." She leaned in closer and lowered her voice. "Was he good looking?"

I leaned toward her and matched my tone to hers. "Very."

"Is he as handsome as our new police chief?"

I coughed, and she laughed.

"Lucky you."

"Oh, no, we're not—"

"Mmmhmm. Everyone sees the way you two look at each other. Way more sparks than Reed's crazy weather machine could ever make."

There were seriously no secrets in Wishville. My face flushed.

She grinned. "What can I help you with today, hon."

I cleared my throat, happy to change the subject. "I need access to the notes from the historic zoning commission's spring meeting. Something about a redevelopment plan near the wishing well."

She blinked. "That meeting was so boring I spent half of it drawing cupcakes in the margins. What are you looking for?"

"Proof that Henry McAlister is a liar." I held up a bag of lemon poppyseed muffins I'd baked as an incentive to let me take a peek.

She tilted her head like a curious cat, inhaled the delicious aroma, and then wordlessly gestured to the wall of ancient metal filing cabinets. My father's house wasn't the only thing that needed modernization.

Wishville itself was stuck in the past.

"Fifth drawer down," she said. "You didn't see me help you. Also—cupcakes weren't metaphorical. Page six."

I rifled through the folder, flipping past dry legal language and passive-aggressive side comments about delayed permits. Sure enough, Amanda's cupcakes danced cheerfully along the edge of the April meeting notes. The one meeting I hadn't been able to make because I'd been in Elarion at a different Council meeting.

I scanned the attendees list—Mayor Hemsworth, Assistant Mayor Delaney, Samuel Greer, Rowan Baxter, two business owners...but no Henry McAlister. No comment recorded. No line item about his "passionate presentation," which he'd bragged about at the Founders' Day BBQ like he was the next urban visionary.

"Gotcha," I muttered, snapping a photo with my phone. I handed Amanda the bag of muffins.

She accepted them as if she were stocking up for winter. "Bless you, my friend. Now go solve whatever mess you're in the middle of before you drag the squirrels into it."

As I exited the building, Holden was waiting in the parking lot. He was leaning against his cruiser, his sport coat collar popped against the wind, one coffee in each hand, and a permanent scowl in place.

He really was one ruggedly, handsome man.

I blinked. Where had that thought come from? Shaking my brain back into saner thoughts, I said, "Morning."

"You get what you needed?"

I held up my phone. "No record of Henry McAlister attending that meeting. No speech, no support, just cupcakes."

Holden raised a brow. "Cupcakes?"

"Don't ask."

He handed me one of the coffees and then opened the door to

the cruiser for me. I thanked him and slid inside, then he shut my door and climbed in the other side. The air was already toasty from the heater. Early morning springtime in the mountains of Vermont could be downright cold. The scent of leather, wintergreen gum, and faint pine cleaner filled the cab.

"I've got something too," he said, pulling out his phone and tapping through a few emails. "I went through Samuel's work correspondence again this morning. Guess who sent him three 'friendly' messages about the redevelopment project?"

"Henry," I answered.

"Bingo. Two were harmless, but the third offered him a 'consulting bonus' to change his position."

"So, a bribe." Anger filled me over the lengths some people would go to ruin WishFest.

"Yup. A slick, overly polite one dressed up like a job offer."

"Let me guess, Samuel never responded. He didn't care about money. He cared about preserving history and proving legends." Or at least I hoped he did.

"Exactly. But that didn't stop Henry's crew from drafting maps. One of the construction foremen turned over a few blueprints showing a proposed access road that runs directly next to the wishing well. Practically crushes the western side of the clearing."

"That would destroy the grove. I wouldn't put it past him to have his crew do something to tap into the water source that fills the well. That might be why it is drying up." It was either that or Samuel's wish was doing even more damage than we thought.

"Which means no more festival. No more tourists. No more money." Holden shrugged. "Look, I'll be honest. I still think having the festival so often is a bad idea. I'm just doing my job by trying to solve a murder and keep everyone safe."

"Fair enough, even though I'm still determined to change your mind." I stared out the window as the town passed by in a blur. "So maybe that's what this is about," I said. "If someone wanted the festival to die, the easiest way to kill it would be to kill the well."

McAlister Construction looked exactly like the kind of place that wanted to convince you it was "local" while funneling cash to out-of-state investors. The building was all fake charm—distressed barnwood paneling, a metal awning painted to look rusted, and flower boxes filled with unnervingly perfect fake ivy.

Inside, the lobby was sterile and over-decorated, like someone Googled "cozy industrial chic" and bought every item in the top results. The receptionist—auburn hair, glassy-eyed, and dressed in business casual so sharp it could cut glass—offered us a cold smile.

"Mr. McAlister is expecting you."

She gestured down a hallway lined with framed renderings of housing developments and shiny apartment complexes. One showed a sleek modern plaza where the well clearing should've been, complete with a suspiciously chipper juice bar and a "reflective water feature" that looked like a glorified puddle.

Holden grunted. "Subtle."

We were ushered into a corner office. Henry McAlister stood behind a glass desk, his too-white teeth gleaming under overhead lights. His suit looked like it cost more than my car, and his handshake was just firm enough to register without sincerity.

"Lyra Wells! Chief Thorn," he boomed. "To what do I owe this pleasure?" His voice oozed fake charm like hot syrup over a freezer-burned pancake, making me wonder what else he was hiding.

"We're here about Samuel Greer," Holden said, his voice clipped. "And your correspondence with him."

Henry gestured toward two glossy leather chairs. "Of course, of course. Terrible what happened. I was just saying the other day what a loss he was to the community."

"You told several people you spoke at the spring zoning meeting," I said, "but you weren't there."

Henry chuckled like I'd made a silly mistake. "I must've

mixed up the dates. I've been involved in so many discussions lately."

"And emails," I added, trying to keep my cool. "Including one where you offered Samuel money to change his stance on your redevelopment plan."

"That was misinterpreted," he said smoothly. "It was a consulting role—entirely aboveboard. I simply wanted his expertise."

"You also conveniently neglected to mention the proposed road," Holden added.

Henry's smile didn't falter. "We hadn't finalized that proposal."

I stepped closer, meeting his gaze directly and struggling to stay calm. "The wishing well is drying up."

His smile froze. A muscle near his left eye twitched, just for a second. "That's unfortunate," he said lightly. "Perhaps it's a seasonal thing."

"No, Henry," I said, "it's not. Something is disrupting the well's flow. The water levels are at an all-time low. And people are noticing, too. I even heard a few of them worry their wishes might not come true if it dries up.

He rolled his eyes. "The wishes coming true are from the power of suggestion, not magic." He shrugged. "If the well is no longer a viable resource for the town, then it may be time to rethink the land's use. Progress waits for no one."

Holden leaned in. "Is that what you said to Samuel…right before you used Reed's prototype on him to stop him?"

I was surprised Holden would reveal that information to McAlister…unless he wanted to test his knowledge and look for a reaction.

"I don't know what you're talking about." Henry's expression remained masked, making it impossible to tell what he was thinking. "If you'll excuse me, I have another meeting." He stood, already dismissing us. "I assure you that I've done nothing wrong. I only want what's best for Wishville."

"Funny," I said, rising and turning toward the door, my palms clenching into fists. "Sounds to me like you want what's best for you, and somehow that always seems to involve tearing down what everyone else loves."

Holden and I left without another word. Outside, the fog had lifted slightly, revealing the ridge line above town. I looked up toward the distant woods, where the well sat like a weakening heartbeat beneath the trees.

"He's hiding something," I said.

"No doubt," Holden muttered.

I nodded, thinking, the well wasn't just drying up. It was being *choked*. And if Henry was behind it, then we weren't just dealing with a developer...

We were dealing with someone who was trying to erase magic one blueprint at a time.

If there was one name that could make the Historical Society groan and the Parks Department reach for their stress balls, it was Gavin Rhoades. "Rogue archaeologist" was his self-assigned title. Everyone else just called him *the guy with a PhD in Delusions who tried to dig up Elarion in someone's petunia bed*. It was my job to make sure people believed Elarion to be nothing more than a fairytale, so I always played along.

We parked just off the old forestry access road that curved around Hollow Glen. The gravel crackled under the tires as Holden cut the engine.

It was nearly noon now, and a layer of morning mist still clung to the forest floor, curling around tree roots like sleepy tendrils. Usually, it had burned off by now. Overhead, the canopy of birch and maple filtered the weak sunlight into soft, pale stripes across the ground. The woods smelled like damp bark, wet leaves, and the faint metallic tang of something disturbed.

In the back seat, Vex let out a long, dramatic sigh and curled deeper into the sweater I brought in case the chill didn't lift. He'd insisted on tagging along but clearly had decided rogue archaeologists weren't worth his time. Holden and I climbed out of the cruiser and made our way on foot.

"You sure this is the trail?" he asked, eyeing the narrow footpath ahead with trepidation.

"Positive. According to three separate complaint logs to the Forest Ranger's State Parks Department, someone's been trespassing around here for weeks—digging, mumbling, stealing bark. Samuel is dead. And unless there's a second eccentric who believes Elarion is buried beneath Wishville, this is Gavin's domain."

Not to mention my Seismic Sense was leading the way,

"Fantastic. Another obsessed psychopath," Holden muttered, checking the safety on his sarcasm.

We hiked in silence, our boots crunching softly on the leaf-strewn path. The air grew cooler as we descended into the hollow, shadows lengthening between the trees. Birdsong chirped overhead, but even that sounded tentative like the forest was holding its breath.

Halfway up the ridge that bordered the crater site, I spotted it —a scuffed footprint in the mud. Fresh, deep, and too big to be mine. Too heavy to be recent hiker traffic, either.

I crouched. "Someone's been here within the last twenty-four hours."

Holden scanned the underbrush. "And not hiding it."

Branches snapped to our left. We turned the corner of a boulder-strewn hill, and there it was...Gavin Rhoades' campsite. If an explosion of red string, caffeine, and eccentricity could take physical form, it would look exactly like this tent.

A sagging dome of duct-taped nylon leaned between two trees, surrounded by a chaotic sprawl of half-crumpled maps, flagged soil samples, and empty Red Bull cans stacked like sacrificial offerings to the gods of overstimulation. A solar-powered radio hummed static beside a rusty shovel. And a hand-drawn poster titled *VEINS OF MAGIC: FIELD NOTES, VOL. 6* flapped in the breeze from a tree branch.

We stepped closer, and just then, the tent flap flew open. Gavin stumbled out in mismatched hiking boots, a field notebook clutched in one hand, and a dirty toothbrush in the other like a dagger.

"Aha!" he cried. "The frequency predicted your arrival! The soil told me someone skeptical was coming."

Gavin Rhoades looked like Indiana Jones' over-caffeinated cousin. Mid-forties, wiry as a ferret, with wild curls that defied gravity and smudges of dirt under every fingernail. His coat was long and moth-eaten, and his socks—visible above his boots— were bright neon and likely unwashed.

"Gavin," I said, "you're digging without a permit." I glanced around, looking for more marks and wondering if any rebel Dwellers might be nearby.

He looked deeply wounded. "I'm *communing* with the land, Lyra. Excavation implies force. I am listening to the whispers of geological memory."

Holden rubbed his temple. "You're trespassing *again*. You were formally barred from this area after Samuel turned you in for unlicensed activity."

"Tragic business, Samuel." Gavin waved a hand. "Brilliant man. A little too...rule-bound, but he had vision."

I stepped on a branch that snapped.

Gavin pivoted toward me suddenly, his eyes wide and feverbright. "Lyra, the energy out here since the cold snap...it's changed. I was in a different part of the woods but then I felt a new energy vibrating in the roots. There's a resonance now. A pull. I followed the energy, and it led me here. The crater is a signal. I'm *so* close to locating Elarion. It's real, you know. Not just a legend." His words came in quick, excited bursts, like he couldn't get them out fast enough.

Oh, *I* knew Elarion was real, but no one else would know it existed for sure or its location if I had anything to say about it. "Still chasing the lost city?" I asked, keeping my tone light.

"I'm not *chasing*. I'm following the signs." He motioned to a chalk circle drawn on the ground beside his tent. "That symbol appeared in the soil near the burn line. It's not natural, not recent, and *not from this world*."

Holden raised a brow. "Did the soil also suggest your snack options? Because there's a lot of Red Bull out here."

"Don't mock the sacred elixir," Gavin replied. "Sleep dulls perception."

I left Holden to duel with Gavin's logic and wandered toward the far side of the camp, where a pit had been dug—roughly six feet wide, three feet deep, and lined with hand-labeled stakes. My boots crunched over pebbles as I crouched beside it, brushing my hand across the soil.

It was warm. Not sun-warm, not cozy-earth-warm—*unnaturally* warm. There were faint shimmering layers in the soil, like someone had disturbed it with heat, and now the ground hadn't recovered.

"Feel this," I called.

Holden joined me and pressed a hand to the earth. His brow furrowed. "That's not right," he muttered.

"Exactly. Reed Callahan's prototype is supposed to manipulate temperature fluctuations. What if this was his test site? Or what if someone stole it and tried to recreate something here?"

Behind us, Gavin cleared his throat dramatically and emerged with something in his hands. "For your safety," he declared, "I present to you *the portal-finder hat!*" He held it out to Holden with great reverence. It was an unholy creation of tinfoil, feathers, and what looked like a broken spaghetti strainer hot-glued to a headband.

Portal? I swallowed hard, hoping Holden wouldn't pick up on that.

Holden stared at it like it was radioactive. "If I wear that, does it summon backup or commit me?"

"You'll be grateful." Gavin stared at him with bloodshot eyes that looked as if they hadn't closed in days. "It protects your brainwaves from inversion bleed. Ask the crows. They know."

"I think I'll pass." Holden delicately placed the hat on a stump like it might detonate.

I stifled a laugh and straightened. "Gavin, did you ever talk to Reed about the prototype?"

Gavin nodded solemnly. "Once. He dismissed me. Said I was, quote, 'playing mad scientist in a sandbox full of delusions.' But I know he was hiding something. His shed was locked up tight."

Holden blinked. "You tried to break into Reed Callahan's shed?"

"Only *once*," Gavin admitted, "but I was repelled by a weathervane that spat Latin insults at me."

I couldn't tell if that was real or the result of too much Red Bull and feather glue, but I added it to my mental file anyway. We circled the pit again, scanning for signs of equipment or buried components. The area was disturbingly quiet, even the wind seemed reluctant to stir now. The energy here was *wrong*—subtle, but wrong.

Like something remained unfinished.

As we turned back toward the trail, Gavin called after us. "You'll see! Elarion will be discovered, and everyone will finally know I'm not crazy!"

Holden glanced at me. "Does he actually believe that?"

"Every word," I said, rolling my eyes, but secretly trying not to panic. Gavin Rhoades was *not* crazy. He was actually a brilliant man who was far too close to the truth.

Holden's eyebrows pinched together. "What do you think he would do if he found Reed's prototype?"

"He'd use it," I replied immediately, "whether it worked or not just to prove a point."

Holden exhaled slowly. "He's unstable, not stupid. That makes him dangerous."

I looked back once at the smudged outlines of Gavin's maps

flapping on the trees like warnings. "If he didn't create the crater," I said softly, "he's certainly trying to replicate it." Or find another portal. If anyone could create a new way into Elarion, it would be a genius like Gavin Rhoades.

I suddenly realized solving Samuel's murder, saving the drying well, and keeping the treaty intact might not be the only things we had to worry about.

Elarion might be in more trouble than I thought.

CHAPTER
Twelve

LATE AFTERNOON SUNLIGHT streamed through the warped panes of my kitchen windows, casting slats across the worn wood floor. The scent of chamomile tea still lingered in the air, though it had long gone cold beside a stack of haphazard town records, a pile of notes, and a half-eaten ginger snap.

Calderis had checked in on me with the orb, which he never did unless there was an emergency, making me think he might actually be jealous. I filled him in on Gavin, and he promised to beef up security around the portal entrance as a precaution.

I sat cross-legged on the floor, having showered and changed into a clean, soft, comfy maxi dress after our trip to the construction site followed by our hike in the woods. Rebel Dwellers were still present in my mind, but now I was also trying to make sense of my notes on Rowan, Reed, Henry, and Gavin and how they were connected to Samuel Greer.

Could any of them have actually killed him?

And how did the prototype really fit in?

A sound like irritated silk rustling across velvet announced Vex's descent from the windowsill. He slinked into view, his tail twitching and eyes a sharp blend of silver and violet—shifting like dusk over water.

Half mortal cat, half magical Whispen, and full-time critic of my life choices.

"You've been awfully cozy with Holden Thorn lately." He stretched lazily before me. "Tell me, is he the kind of man who brings brooding as a plus-one to dinner?"

I arched an eyebrow, sweeping my multi-colored hair over my shoulder as I nailed him with an amber glare. "Seriously?"

Vex blinked slowly and sauntered closer, inspecting me like I was a piece of produce that had begun to bruise. "You haven't denied it."

I reached out and flicked the soft tip of his tail. "Because it's not true. Holden and I are...friends. That's it."

"Friends," he repeated, curling onto the braided rug with a sigh so theatrical I half-expected a spotlight to appear. "Like I'm just your cat, and the portal to Elarion is *just decorative landscaping*."

"We're working together on the case. You know how important this is." I leaned my head against the cabinet, my eyes drifting to the ceiling. "Samuel's murder has stalled the entire seasonal cycle. His unauthorized early wish is still in the well, clogging the magic like old hair in a drain. If we don't clear it by the end of WishFest, the well won't choose a recipient, and—"

"—the treaty fractures, the energy balance unravels, and all chaos breaks loose," Vex finished, rolling onto his back with his paws in the air. "Yes, I've been alive for over four lifetimes, thank you. I *do* read the memos."

I couldn't help smiling, despite the knot in my chest. "Then you know Holden is simply trying to help. He doesn't believe in magic or the legend, he's just doing his job. Keeping the town safe."

Vex righted himself with a huff. "He smells like whiskey, and he looks at you like you're one bad decision away from giving him a heart attack."

Before I could argue, my phone rang on the counter. I reached up and swiped it, already knowing who it would be.

Holden Thorn.

"Hey," I said, tucking a strand of hair behind my ear.

"Hey," he said back, his voice the same low rumble I'd grown used to—gritty, calm, a little tired. "You eat yet?"

"Just emotional cookies." I glanced guiltily at the open tin.

"You call that food?"

"I call it coping."

He chuckled. "Meet me at *The Wishing Lounge*? I want to go over my case notes. Might be easier in person."

"Sure. Fifteen minutes?"

"Works for me."

As I ended the call, I turned to find Vex watching me with narrowed eyes.

"Just friends, huh?" he muttered, arching his back in disdain. "Let me know when he starts braiding your hair."

I tossed a dish towel in his general direction. "Be good while I'm gone."

"Oh, honey, I'm the cat's meow."

The Wishing Lounge Bar and Grill sat on the edge of downtown, perched like a cozy woodland tavern with artfully crooked shingles and flickering stained-glass sconces. A sign carved from driftwood swung gently in the breeze, and the window boxes were bursting with trailing ivy and midnight-blue petunias.

Inside, it smelled like spiced booze and rosemary fries, with the low thrum of folk music playing over the speakers. The booths were patched leather, and the ceiling was strung with twinkling lights that gave the place the illusion of being dipped in starlight.

Holden sat at a high-top table in the corner, wearing clean jeans and a soft-looking dark green shirt that hugged his muscles, no sport coat in sight. He looked up as I approached, standing in that quiet, brooding way of his. His dark buzzed hair was slightly damp, and his beard neatly trimmed. He looked and smelled amazing. A rugged man with a musky mix of bourbon and the outdoors.

Vex's hissing laughter whispered through my brain.

I frowned and looked away.

"You look...different," Holden blurted.

"So do you," I seconded and tried not to blush.

"I ordered fries," he said, clearing his throat. "Figured you'd need them."

"Fries are my love language," I replied, sliding into the chair opposite him, and then blinked. Had I really just said that out loud? *Friends, Lyra, just friends.*

We hadn't even gotten past the pleasantries when I noticed Evelyn Poe gliding through the doors. Her coat was cream-colored and belted tightly, like she was bracing herself against the world. She scanned the bar, spotted us, and beelined in our direction like a missile wearing lipstick.

"I see the gossip train rolls on," she said, her eyes flashing. "I can't even eat dinner without you two circling me like vultures?" She tucked her shoulder-length brown hair behind her ears.

"It's a free country, Ms. Poe. We came for dinner as well, not to mention, we were here first." Holden didn't so much as flinch. "And might I remind you you're still a person of interest after the way you stalked Samuel."

Her mouth twisted. "You mean I'm guilty until proven innocent."

I tried to keep my voice even. "You told us you and Samuel met on *EverAfter*, but he said he never swiped right. You didn't match him. You know I heard him tell you exactly that."

"But I did. The app doesn't lie." She raised her chin. "He found me. He knew who I was and said things no stranger could've guessed."

"Such as?" Samuel must have deleted his account because there was no record of one anywhere to be found. Because of this, we had no notes for what was actually said between them...unless we could take a peek at hers.

She hesitated. "Sacred things that no one else would understand."

"The solution is simple," Holden said. "Show us your phone."

Her eyes widened, and she was already shaking her head. "I can't. I deleted the messages. They were far too personal."

How convenient, I thought. "Deleted the messages before or after he ghosted you? And yet you came to Wishville anyway." I watched her closely.

She crossed her arms, ignoring my question. "He loved me, he just wouldn't admit it."

Holden folded his hands on the table. "You realize people reported you loitering outside his cottage and his work. We have footage."

And I saw her, I thought.

She paled. "That's...that's not stalking. I was trying to reach him. He *wanted* me to."

"Did he tell you that?" I asked gently.

Her jaw clenched. "He didn't have to. I felt it. He was scared, that's all."

"And yet he stopped responding and blocked your number," Holden said.

Evelyn's breath caught. "Because he was afraid, but not of me. Of *us* and what we could've been. He led me on, made promises, and then acted like I was crazy."

Holden's voice turned firm and full of authority. "Don't leave town, Ms. Poe. This isn't over."

She looked at both of us and her eyes changed, filling with pure venom. "I gave up everything to come here. Everything! And he threw me away like garbage." Then she turned on her heel and stormed out, the click of her sandals echoing through the lounge.

The fries arrived seconds later.

"Appetizer with a side of rage," I muttered, pushing the basket toward Holden.

"She's unstable," he said. "Could be grief or maybe guilt, but either way, she's hiding something."

We finished our fries in silence, no longer having an appetite for dinner, and then stepped outside. The air smelled of honeysuckle, and a chorus of frogs chirped somewhere in the distance. The town felt almost enchanted under the purpling sky.

Then we saw it.

A small black notebook lay half-buried in the grass by the curb, its leather cover gleaming faintly. Holden crouched and picked it up, frowning at the embossed initials. "E.P.," he murmured, flipping it open, and then handing it to me wordlessly.

~ Samuel brushed my hand when he gave me change at the antique store. I think he felt it too. The spark. The soul-link.

~ He's pulling away. He's probably scared, or someone is warning him. They always try to keep me from happiness.

~ He locked the door again today, but I saw him peek through the curtains. He misses me. He's just not brave enough.

Then the entries darkened, both literally and figuratively.

~ If he rejects me again, I'll show him what heartbreak really feels like. He'll pay for leading me on if it's the last thing I do.

My fingers tightened around the leather. "She's delusional."

"She's dangerous," Holden said quietly, "and this could be motive."

I looked up at him, the hair on my arms rising in the fading light. "This could be proof."

The scent of sugar and yeast warmed my insides as I stepped into *The Twisted Loaf*. The bell above the door gave a cheerful jingle, announcing my arrival to the quiet crowd already nestled in booths and chairs, sipping lattes and catching up on local gossip.

Cinnamon, baking bread, and the faint trace of roasted espresso drifted past my nose, making my mouth water. It was the kind of cozy that made you forget for a moment that a murderer might still be wandering around town.

Calderis was growing restless with my orb updates, insisting I come back to Elarion and talk to him in person soon. I smiled over the memory, and then frowned. What was wrong with me? I shook my head and then spotted Holden.

He sat at a table near the stone hearth, his sport coat draped over the back of his chair. He looked tired. His normal perfectly crisp dress shirt was slightly wrinkled, his tie a little lop-sided, his badge clipped crookedly to his belt, and his cup of coffee already half gone. A small paper bag sat in front of him, grease-stained and dusted with powdered sugar.

"Morning." I slipped into the seat across from him and pulled my coat tighter. The breeze outside had been brisk, hinting that summer was still a long way off.

"Hope you like blackberry scones," he said without looking up. "They were the last ones. I nearly lost a finger to an old man."

I opened the bag and breathed in the warm, buttery scent. "Blackberry scones are my favorite. You keep earning brownie points."

"I'm more of a biscuit guy." He took a sip of black coffee.

Before I could respond, Betsy Plum came sweeping by in her bread-themed apron, a smudge of flour on her chin, and the energy of someone who'd already had three cups of coffee too many.

"Well, if it isn't Sherlock and his little Watson." She beamed. "Coffee's got a cinnamon stick in it today, Lyra. You'll like it—it's got vision. Might open your third eye."

"I'll settle for keeping the two I have open," I replied with a smile.

She patted Holden on the shoulder—he stiffened slightly— and she winked at me. "Don't let him hog the good table forever. I've got a book club staking it out for 10:30." With that, she bustled off, leaving us in a quiet little bubble of warm pastries and unspoken tension.

Holden waited until Betsy was out of earshot before leaning in. "We found something last night hidden near the well."

I blinked, halfway through a bite of the scone. "Hidden?"

"Wedged into the rocks near the base of the stone pillar on the eastern side. Someone had taped it underneath the ledge. We almost missed it. It was partially damaged, but we managed to recover some of the information."

"What was it?"

"A voice recorder." He slid his phone across the table. "And it belongs to Marin Holloway."

I froze. "The journalist from *The Wish Weekly*?"

"The very one."

I wiped my hands on a napkin, my heart thudding. "What's on it?" I tried not to freak out as I struggled to remember what exactly Vex and I had said out loud. Most of our conversations were done through our minds, but still...

He tapped his screen and brought up an audio clip. It was short, crackling with static, but clear enough that I could make out Samuel's voice—low, excited, and breathless. "I finally have proof. The portal is—" The recording ended abruptly, like someone had shut it off mid-revelation, or something had damaged it.

I stared at the phone, chills creeping down my spine. He was about to say something about Elarion. I donned an innocent expression. "Portal?" Between the memory crystal and the recording, more pieces of the puzzle surrounding Samuel's death were being revealed.

Holden shrugged. "That's what it sounded like."

"Was there anything else on the recording?"

"No, that was it. I think he was as crazy as Reed, but that's not the point." His gaze met mine. "Marin didn't mention anything about a recording when we questioned her earlier."

"So, she either forgot...or she didn't want us to know."

He stood and grabbed his jacket. "Let's find out which."

I followed him outside.

The walk to *The Wish Weekly* took longer than I had anticipated. The building sat on the edge of town in an old, converted feed mill, all red brick and ivy-covered charm, with a hand-painted sign that looked like it hadn't been touched since the late '80s. Inside, it smelled like dust, toner, and yesterday's coffee.

The second-floor newsroom was a cluttered landscape of headlines, stacked newspapers, paperclip towers, and desks that looked like they'd been stolen from different decades. A whirring ceiling fan ticked overhead like a timebomb.

Marin Holloway stood near her desk, tall and sharp-angled, with her brunette hair twisted into a messy knot and a pen tucked behind one ear. She wore a slate-gray button-up and black jeans, her sleeves rolled to the elbows, an ink smudge on her left forearm like a badge of honor.

She looked up as we entered, her eyes flicking between Holden and me. "Well, well. You brought your muse this time."

Holden ignored the jab. "We found a voice recorder near the well, taped to a stone. It's yours."

Her spine stiffened. "That's not possible."

"It had your initials carved on the back," I said, "and Samuel's voice on the tape."

She frowned, reaching for a mug that said *Truth Over Everything*. "I haven't seen that recorder in weeks. It was stolen from my office."

"Did you report it?" Holden asked.

She hesitated. "No. I figured it was long gone. It wasn't expensive."

"Yet someone went through a lot of trouble to stash it by the well," I said.

Marin's fingers tightened on her mug. "I don't know anything about that."

Holden's gaze swept her desk. Among the mess of notebooks and sticky notes was an open planner with scrawled notes and clipped headlines. One page had a scrap of paper tucked beneath it. He reached down and lifted it free before she could snatch it back.

The headline read:

PORTAL TO ELARION CONFIRMED!
Local Scholar Reveals Explosive Truth

My heart skipped a beat. The article wasn't finished—just an outline—but the implication was clear. "You were going to publish this?" I asked.

"Samuel accused you of harassing him," Holden added. "You pressured him into revealing something he wasn't ready to share."

"He promised me an exclusive," she snapped. "He said he'd found proof. That he was ready to expose the truth about the well, the magic, everything. Then he got cold feet."

"And you were angry," I added.

"I was furious!" Marin admitted. "That kind of story? It would've blown everything wide open. I've been chasing myths and festivals and ghost stories for years, waiting for something real. Samuel had it, and then he just...cut me off. He said it was too dangerous, and he had to protect the town."

"So, you what?" Holden asked. "Went after it yourself?"

She folded her arms. "I'm a reporter, not a thief, and definitely not a murderer."

Holden took a slow step forward. "Here's the problem. Someone broke into Samuel's cottage the night after he died. His research notes? Gone. Pages, files, everything. Someone knew exactly what to take."

That knocked the wind out of her. "I—no. That wasn't me."

He didn't blink. "You had motive. You had the recorder. You had the story."

"And now I have a big empty nothing." Her voice cracked slightly. "If I wanted a scoop, I lost it. I lost everything. Don't you get it? I believed him. I believed he had something real, and he made a fool out of me."

We stood there for a beat too long. The air between us filled with the low hum of printers and the ticking of the fan. Then I spotted it—on the wall behind her desk. A photo of Samuel tacked beside a map of Wishville with red threads connecting various locations: Reed's workshop, the crater, the well, the library, the construction site...

Even *my* house.

"She's been tracking more than just Samuel," I whispered.

Marin's eyes darted to the map then back to me. "I told you. I'm a reporter following leads."

Holden stared at her, his expression unreadable. "You're a suspect. Consider that your biggest lead yet."

CHAPTER
Thirteen

THE GARAGE DOOR creaked like rusted scrap metal, making my skin prickle. *Wishville Wheels* was more chaos than commerce —a graveyard of half-repaired classics, scattered tools, and the occasional tire rolling aimlessly.

Rumor had it that Sparks was a long lost relative of the former owner, finally claiming his inheritance of the old shop that had sat abandoned for years. I did *not* want to know what he had done to gain access to the building, but I had to give him credit. That was a pretty good cover.

Grease-stained banners drooped from the ceiling, advertising brands that hadn't been made in twenty years. The scent of oil and singed rubber hit me like a punch to the nose, but underneath it, I caught a flicker of charged air.

Vex slinked beside me, his tail low and fur slightly puffed. He hated this place. I couldn't blame him. It felt unsettled.

"Sparks?" I called, stepping deeper into the shop.

A grunt echoed from beneath a cherry-red '67 Firebird propped on a lift. A moment later, a pair of long legs slid out from under it, followed by a torso slick with sweat and engine grease. Sparks pushed himself upright with a grunt, wiping his brow with the back of his hand, the wrench in his grip still gleaming.

"Well, well." His voice was rough, low, and amused. "Look what the cat dragged in." His eyes flicked to Vex, who arched a single disdainful eyebrow back at him. "Though I'm guessing this visit isn't social."

I crossed my arms. "Not unless you count mild accusations and uncomfortable truths as friendly banter."

Sparks grinned, his teeth white and skin pale beneath his temporary tattoos—part of his disguise. "Sounds like my kind of date." He turned his back and walked toward a rolling workbench, his blonde hair pulled back in a low ponytail. "You want a donut? It's not *Twisted Loaf* worthy, but it's not bad. Cinnamon twist from the gas station next door."

"I'll pass," I said, cutting to the chase. "Holden thinks Marin Holloway broke into Samuel's cottage and stole his research notes."

Sparks snorted, flipping open a drawer with a metallic screech. "Of course he does. The human mind favors simplicity." He plucked out a screwdriver and spun it between his fingers, sending crackles into the air.

"So, you're saying things are more complex than that."

He stilled, slowly turning back to face me. His expression dimmed into something more serious. "Let's skip the flirtation and get to the part where you ask me why I was there."

My throat tightened. "Then you *were* at Samuel's?"

"The night before he died," he said evenly.

The silence in the garage deepened. Even the hum of the fluorescent lights seemed to pause.

I studied him closely. "You didn't tell anyone."

He shrugged. "I'm telling you now."

I took a breath. "Why?"

"Because I found out Samuel had a memory crystal." His voice dropped, rough with frustration. "When I was pulled through the portal, I felt its energy. I tracked it to Samuel and thought he might listen to reason."

"You tried to buy it from him?"

"Barter." He shrugged. "I pretended to collect antiques as well and offered him a relic—a treaty stone from the caverns under Lake Mistfall. A rare find. Something most scholars would slit throats to study."

"And?"

"He didn't believe me. He accused me of being a treasure hunter, saying he had the real deal and wasn't about to part with it. I might have been against the treaty in the past, but that doesn't mean I want Elarion's secrets getting out."

I winced, the weight of the crystal hidden under my floorboards burning hotter in my mind. I'd finally gone back and listened to the other recordings. They were of Dwellers from Elarion, giving away details of Elarion's riches, which would be damaging in the wrong hands. Samuel's was the final recording before it got damaged.

Sparks' gaze met mine as he admitted, "I lost my temper. I yelled and knocked over a lamp, maybe more."

"Did you hurt him?"

"He was alive when I left," Sparks said tightly. "Annoyed, but alive."

"Then how do you explain the scorch marks near the well?"

He raised his eyebrows. "You tell me. I'm not the only one in Wishville with a short fuse and a stake in buried secrets."

The air between us sizzled—unsaid truths charged like static. "You didn't kill him?"

"No," he said, "but someone did, and the crystal is gone." His electric blue gaze sharpened, slashing through me like cold light. "Unless you know something I don't..." He didn't say it. He didn't have to.

He *suspected*.

I kept my voice even. "If I had it, wouldn't I have handed it over to Calderis?"

"Depends." Sparks didn't blink. "You're different. Your human half sometimes stops you from playing by Dweller rules."

I glanced at Vex. He let out a low, vibrating grumble, his eyes narrowed slits.

Sparks stepped back, reaching into a bin of rags and pulling one free. He wiped his hands in slow, deliberate circles, like he was calming himself. "You're wasting time chasing Marin."

"I know," I agreed. "She's a liar but not a killer."

"Exactly. You want to know who silenced Samuel?" He leaned in just enough that I caught the faint scent of motor oil and burnt rubber. "Look at *Thayn*."

I blinked, remembering Calderis's words, but I played dumb, probing to see what Sparks might know. "I thought he was in exile. Off meditating or...whatever the enforcers call spiritual avoidance."

Sparks scoffed. "That's the official line. The truth? He's been riling up dissent in the outer caverns. Preaching rebellion and talking about tearing down the treaty, cleansing the surface world."

Cleansing the surface world? Things were more dire than I thought when it came to the rebels. My chest tightened. "Do you think he's actually here in Wishville?"

"I *know* he is." His voice was flat and hard. "Every time the energy near the crater flickers, that's him testing boundaries, pushing to see if the veil thins enough to create a new portal. Samuel was close to revealing the portal's location to the world. That made him dangerous."

"He wouldn't—" I stopped myself. Of course, Thayn would. He was a zealot. A purist. The kind of Dweller who thought sacrifice was noble if it served a greater good. "What if he's after the crystal too?" I asked. "I'm sure he wouldn't want any humans to have Dweller technology."

Sparks tilted his head. "Then I suggest you keep it far from curious hands."

I said nothing. My silence stretched a little too long.

He didn't press, but the glint in his eye said he'd noticed. "You should be careful, Lyra. Thayn doesn't see you as neutral. He sees you as a mistake. Half-human. A fracture in the old ways, standing in his way moving forward."

The words stung, though they shouldn't have. I'd heard worse. "If he's here," I asked, "how do I find him?"

Sparks gave me a bitter smile. "You don't. *He* finds *you* when he's ready. And if he creates a new portal first, the treaty won't be the only thing that burns."

I didn't reply. I couldn't.

The scent of charcoal was stronger now, burning at the edges of my perception. A storm waiting in the bones of the earth. I turned and walked out, with Vex pressed close at my heel, silent. Outside, the sun was blinding, but it didn't warm me.

Not anymore.

The clearing that housed the festival grounds buzzed like a honeycomb at full bloom.

Sunlight spilled through the canopy of blooming trees, high-lighting the worn path as I stepped over a clump of wild clover and onto the grass. Woodsmoke, grilled sausage, and maple everything permeated the air.

Vendors sold their wares, children dashed between booths with fairy wings and dragon tails pinned to their backs, and someone had clearly mistaken a bubble machine for an industrial fogger. The entrance to the festival looked vaguely like a rave for the supernatural.

Poor Eli had his hands full, trying to shut off the machine that was stuck on high, his black hair and beard looking like Santa Claus under a layer of soap. While Trip wrote tickets that didn't mean anything.

The illusion of joyful chaos did nothing to soothe the chill under my skin.

Vex slinked low at my side, his black fur slicked to his frame and ears flicking with each rustle of movement. His eyes—those unnervingly intelligent iridescent slits—never stopped scanning. His nose twitched as if the wind were speaking a language only he understood.

"He's here," he muttered, low and firm. "Somewhere close."

"Thayn?" I swallowed hard.

He nodded once, barely perceptible. "He's watching and waiting, probably already knowing *you* have it."

My fingers curled reflexively. The memory crystal's absence from my bag didn't matter—it might as well have been hot against my chest.

"He'll come for you next," Vex said grimly. "You know that, don't you?"

I did, and the weight of it was pressing harder with every passing hour. "Go," I told him quietly. "Check the edges of the clearing and see if Fenrin will help. She would do anything for you, even if you're too blind to see that."

"She would do anything to protect Elarion." Vex's tail lashed once. "And as you say...we're just friends." He darted off before I could respond, melting into the shifting blur of festivalgoers and tents, leaving me standing alone.

I took a steadying breath and headed toward the balloon launch.

Weylan's emerald green hot air balloon of the day gleamed like a jewel at the far end of the field, anchored beside a picnic grove just beyond the face painting booth and a woman dressed as a fortune-telling mushroom. His basket, carved with golden scrollwork and shaped like a tiny turret, was grounded for the moment—likely between rides. A line of eager tourists had their phones already out. These bees were on standby.

Weylan stood tall beside it, waving to a couple in matching "Wishes are Magical" t-shirts who were laughing about how they *almost* dropped their phones midflight. He offered them a theatrical bow and twirled his scarf, which today was a shimmering neon green number that matched his bright eyes and trailed dramatically in the breeze like a cape.

When he saw me, his smile didn't falter—but it grew just a fraction tighter. "Lyra!" he called, wiping imaginary soot from his hands. "Here for a ride or just basking in my magnificent aeronautical presence?"

"Neither," I said, stepping closer and lowering my voice as I pulled him aside. "I need answers."

He raised a brow and lowered the volume of his voice to mine. "Answers? I thought we covered everything when I *saved* you. Doesn't that count for something?"

"I already thanked you, and yes, you told me about being a messenger between realms with a balloon tour guide as your cover. What you *didn't* tell me is that you blew your cover with Samuel, didn't you?" It was a hunch, nothing more, but I'd learned to trust my gut over centuries of guarding the well.

For the first time, Weylan's easy smile faltered. Just for a moment, but I caught it. "He mentioned a few things," he said too lightly. "He was good at observing."

"He figured out your cover wasn't just theatrical flair," I pressed. "He knew you were a Dweller, and he threatened to expose you."

Weylan's eyes, usually warm and full of mischief, shuttered slightly. "He...strongly suggested that if I didn't cooperate, he'd give Marin a front-page exposé titled *The Sky Lies*."

"Cooperate how? Was he blackmailing you?"

Weylan glanced away, pretending to straighten a rope coil. "He wanted information about the portal and Elarion. I told him I didn't know anything useful."

"Did you give him the memory crystal as proof that Elarion exists?" I took a guess.

"No!" Weylan turned back sharply, his voice raw. "I didn't even *see* the blasted thing. He said he had something powerful, sure, but he didn't show it to me. I assumed it was nonsense."

"You're a terrible liar."

He winced, brushing wind-tousled hair out of his face. "Okay, fine. I *suspected* he had something like that, but I swear I didn't give it to him. Calderis would have my head on a blade if he even sniffed that I betrayed him by sharing anything about our realm."

Which is why I hadn't revealed that I had the missing memory crystal to Calderis, either. I narrowed my eyes. "You'd do just about anything to keep Calderis from finding out you messed up, wouldn't you?"

He looked like I'd slapped him. "That's not fair."

"It's not wrong."

Before he could respond, a high-pitched gasp cut through the air behind us. "There it is!" Belle shrieked.

"The Emerald Balloon of Prophecy!" Dot added breathlessly, clutching a small polka dot suitcase covered in peeling rune stickers and googly eyes. "I *told* you it was real!"

Weylan turned slowly, muttering under his breath, "No, please not today..."

The Wellies charged forward, decked out in their festival best. Belle wore a glittering shawl with stars, moons, and pigeons stitched in sequins. Dot had a tea-stained lace parasol. And Tilly...well, Tilly wore a colander woven with lavender vines strapped to her head with elastic and carried a basket full of what looked like scones and sage bundles.

"You!" Belle cried, pointing at Weylan. "You're the wizard, aren't you? Take us to Oz!"

Weylan blinked. "The *what* now?"

"We've brought offerings," Tilly said cheerfully, pulling out a dented thermos labeled *Potion of Courage* and handing it over. "Also snacks."

"I brought a map of Kansas," Dot said proudly, pushing her massive glasses back in place. "Just in case."

"And we've decided," Belle added, "that even if we can't find Toto, we'll still take on the Wicked Witch for what her flying monkeys did to poor Lyra. We're brave like that."

Weylan looked at me, completely helpless. "Why are they like this?"

"They had a sugar-high premonition after my crater episode,

and I specifically remember them talking about watching *The Wizard of Oz* the other day."

He let out a long, suffering sigh when it was clear they weren't leaving without a ride and began helping them into the basket, dodging shawls and ducking flying knitting needles.

"We're off to see the Wizard!" Dot sang.

"Which one?" Tilly whispered. "The one with the electric blue eyes?"

"Who cares. He's sizzling hot." Belle snickered. "He can fly my monkey any day."

As Weylan wrestled with the balloon ropes and a stray broomstick one of them insisted was for navigation, I stepped back and scanned the festival.

The colors were still vivid and the music still played, but my gut filled with growing unease. Somewhere out there, beneath the laughter and lanterns, a Dweller bent on destruction was already moving toward me.

And magic—no matter how sparkly the packaging—was about to get deadly.

CHAPTER
Fourteen

I STOOD at the edge of the wishing well under a sky littered with stars. The soft drone of music and laughter from the festival had faded into the hush of midnight, replaced by Crickets singing their nightly lullaby. A breeze passed over my head as I stared down at the water deep in the well, alarmingly low these days.

Vex stood beside me, his tail lashing low. His eyes, turquoise and silver today, gleamed in the dark. "You don't have to do this tonight," he said.

"I do," I whispered. "The well is drying up, the festival is half over, and we're running out of time." I closed my eyes and said the incantation, then stepped over the edge.

The breathtaking rush of magic coursed through me as I hit bottom and emerged into a subterranean wonder that always stole my breath. This time I headed away from the Council of Elders' chamber, in search of one particular Enforcer.

Bioluminescent trees arched high overhead, their translucent leaves glowing in blues and purples that swayed without wind. The path beneath my slippers shimmered with crushed quartz, and silver mist curled through the air like drifting song. Crystalized vines clung to the walls like frozen flame, and waterfalls of liquid light cascaded into pools that rippled with memories rather than reflections.

This area of the realm smelled of cool stone and stardust and something faintly floral—like orchids that only bloomed under moonlight. My heart ached with how impossibly beautiful and dangerous Elarion was. Everything here was built on balance, and we were dangerously close to toppling it.

"We need to find Calderis," I said.

Vex nodded and took the lead. As a half-mortal creature, he wasn't always welcome in Elarion, either. Tonight, he was quiet and focused as if he felt the shift too. We didn't go far before a figure appeared beneath an arch of flowering stone.

"Lyra," Drelian said, his tone respectful but wary.

He stood tall in a sleeveless vest, embroidered with copper thread and bone-colored beads, and trousers tucked into boots, his pale hair bound in a warrior's braid. No robes today. The staff in his hand glowed faintly at the tip, casting long shadows behind him.

"Drelian." I nodded once. "I need to speak with Calderis right now. It's important."

"He's preparing for meditation," Drelian said, studying me, "but I'll take you."

The *Enforcer's Sanctum* lay nestled in the heart of a crystal grove. The walls of the great hall rose like carved obsidian, flecked with gold veins that pulsed in tandem with the leylines. A basin fire crackled in the center, its flames blue-white and oddly still, as if even the fire respected the sacred silence of this place.

Calderis stood before the flame, cloaked in robes of deep midnight trimmed in cobalt. His hair, silver as moonlight, drifted behind him with the grace of flowing water, though the chamber was still. He turned as we approached.

"I was beginning to wonder if I would see you again. It's been a while," he said quietly, his expression unreadable. "What happened?"

I stepped forward and pulled the memory crystal from my

robes. It was heavier than before, warmer—like it had been feeding on my secrets. "I found this the night Samuel died," I said, my voice catching, "and I didn't tell anyone...not even you."

His face hardened. The fire behind him flared as he softly said in barely more than a whisper, "You kept it from me?"

I decided to be honest. "I got in my head and started to doubt who I could trust up there or down here." I swallowed the lump rising in my throat. "I'm sorry, Calderis. I should have come sooner. I just...I needed to be sure."

The silence between us stretched, taut and humming.

"Crystals are special to our world," he said finally. "They hold power, influence, and great risk over the information recorded on them. If any of them fall into the wrong hands..."

"I know."

He reached out, and I placed the crystal in his palm. It pulsed once and then went still, as if recognizing its rightful guardian. "I'll bring it to the *Chamber of Preservation* to be repaired and restored."

"I wanted to protect it until I had all my answers," I said softly, "but I see now that hiding it only made things worse."

He didn't answer for a moment. Then, without looking at me, he said, "Trust, once fractured, takes more than apologies to mend."

I felt the sting of that, but I deserved it. "There's more," I said. "Sparks tried to barter the crystal from Samuel, but you were right. The one we really need to worry about is Thayn."

His eyes flicked to mine, sharp and alert. "You've seen him?"

"Not yet, but Vex felt him. Sparks did, too. I think he's in Wishville, waiting and watching for the right time to strike. He wanted the crystal." I paused a beat. "I think he's looking for a way to break the treaty for good."

Calderis stepped back from the flame. "If he's broken through the veil..."

"I really think he has," I said. "And he's dangerous, but as I told you in my updates I'm not facing him alone. Chief Thorn is helping me. He doesn't believe the legend is real, but he *does* believe in justice. He's keeping the surface world from falling apart."

Calderis considered that, the hard lines of his face relaxing slightly. "Then you'll have support from both sides."

"Good," I said, relieved that he would be helping me as well, "because I think it's going to take all three of us to succeed."

He nodded once. "Drelian."

The other Dweller stepped silently forward from the shadows.

"Begin a perimeter sweep," Calderis ordered. "Check the outer caverns. If Thayn is still in Elarion stirring unrest, he won't be able to hide for long."

With a nod, Drelian vanished into the glowing mist as silent as stone.

"There's one more person," I added, having given thought to who else might have caused the scorch marks. Who else might be a rebel Dweller. "Maelin might know more than she lets on. As the Flame Keeper of Echo Caverns, she would have felt if there had been a disruption to the elemental cycle. And she has the ability to leave scorch marks like the ones by the well."

Calderis's expression shifted, looking concerned. "Maelin guards more secrets than flames, but she may speak to you. Come."

We descended into the volcanic tunnels of the *Echo Caverns*, where the air shimmered with heat and every footstep returned in whispers. The walls here weren't crystal. They were charred stone, streaked with glowing veins of magma that moved like slow, molten rivers.

Maelin's chamber was a cathedral of fire. Fissures in the rock spewed narrow tongues of flame that danced in rhythmic spirals around the central dais. The flames cast flickering shadows along the walls, revealing murals of long-forgotten elemental rites.

She stood among them, tall and regal, cloaked in crimson and bronze. Her eyes glowed like hot coals, and her copper hair was braided into a crown that sparked with every movement. Heat shimmered from her skin in waves. She could shape fire into emotion-based forms like sparks of anger and flickers of love, and her Resonant Flame power linked flame and sound, carrying one's voice through stone tunnels.

"Calderis," she said coolly, "and the girl of two worlds."

I stepped forward. "We need answers."

"Don't we all." She turned her gaze to the flickering flame above the altar. "You come to blame me for the slow change that's happening to the well."

"We come to ask what you felt," Calderis said.

"The balance is broken," she admitted. "The wish cycle has stuttered. Fire no longer flows to its proper season."

"The well is drying up," I admitted, drawing both their eyes.

"Because of Samuel?" Calderis asked.

"Because he meddled," she snapped before I could speak another word, "and because someone allowed him to." The flames behind her crackled violently at her words.

"Did you kill him?" I asked.

She turned to me fully now, her expression calm but unreadable. "No, but I felt his death in my marrow like a flare in the leylines. And yes—the flames here grew wild that night. That doesn't mean I caused them."

"Then why the scorch marks on your cloak?"

"Fire seeks air," she said, "and the boundary has thinned. I admit that, since the crack in the portal, I walk the borders to keep the burn from spilling over." Her cloak swayed slightly as she moved, and I caught a glimpse of its hem—blackened and curling with ash.

Calderis stepped closer. "You need to be honest with us, Maelin. The treaty depends on it."

She folded her arms. "The treaty depends on many things, including mortals not forcing our hands. But I will give you this— Samuel's actions sparked more than curiosity. They lit a fuse. Not everyone in Elarion is happy with the treaty, even if they are afraid to voice their concerns out loud, just ask Orielle. She said as much to me, though she wouldn't name names. Now, we wait to see where the fire leads." She turned away, dismissing us with the wave of her hand. The flames dimmed, but in the shadows beyond the altar, something still flickered.

And I had the sinking feeling it wasn't done burning.

The path to Orielle's *Sanctuary* twinkled with twilight hues, though Elarion had no sun or moon to guide it—only the realm's ambient light, sensitive to emotion. Tonight, the walls glowed, reflecting our unease with a muted kind of compassion. As we walked, the warmth of the stone beneath my slippers and the low pulse beneath it reminded me that even in fear, there was still life.

"She'll know," I said softly. "Orielle always knows."

Calderis walked beside me, his steps measured and shoulders tight. "Orielle is cautious, and for good reason. She hears what was never meant to be spoken. If she chooses to share anything, it's because she's already calculated the weight of consequence."

Vex padded ahead, his tail swishing as always. "She's partial to Lyra. I can smell it. She dreams of trees and rain and red berries when she's near her."

"She smells?" I asked, trying not to smile.

"She smells of happiness and peace," Vex muttered. "So, pay attention."

We rounded a bend and passed through *Orielle's Sanctuary* into the wide, echoing approach to the *Chamber of Whispers*—where unspoken desires had been captured and stored for generations. It consisted of a domed hall with delicate threads of glowing script that looped and glistened across the walls like a tapestry of memory. Every step here was quieter, as if the stone itself hushed you out of reverence.

Before we could reach the archway, movement near one of the branching alcoves caught our attention. Three figures stood in a soft pool of light: Calderis's mother Elanith, his younger sister

Lumira, and the Ice Seer Selvi, whose presence always felt like the moment before snow began to fall.

"Mother," Calderis said softly, his steps slowing.

Elanith turned at the sound of his voice and smiled, the lines at the corners of her eyes deepening with genuine warmth. Her robe of layered sea-glass blue shimmered like moonlit water, and her silver hair was pinned back with polished pieces of obsidian. When her gaze found me, it softened further.

"Lyra Wells," she said kindly. "It's good to see you safe."

I blinked at her gentle tone, caught off-guard by the warmth behind it. "Thank you." I dipped my head once.

"And you, Mother," Calderis said, bowing.

Lumira stepped beside Elanith, her curls braided and tucked with small blossoms that pulsed faintly with bioluminescent light. She looked like calm fire—bright, but warm.

"We heard about Samuel," Lumira said, her expression solemn. "Is it true his wish is still echoing?"

"That's what we're trying to learn now," I said. "We think Orielle might be able to help."

"You're walking dangerous ground," Selvi said, her voice the brittle hush of cracking frost, "but necessary. I've seen what waits if the echoes are left unanswered." Her pale eyes turned distant and unfocused. "Flames in the well. Frost in places that should never freeze. A shattering between worlds."

Elanith stepped forward and touched Calderis's arm gently. "We know the burden you carry, but you're not your father, Calderis. You don't have to bear it alone."

He nodded, and there was a faint tightening in the line of his jaw.

"And you," she said to me, "you were never an intruder in this realm, Lyra. No matter what anyone else has said. I'm so sorry about your mother. She was a good friend. You carry both worlds in your blood. That doesn't make you dangerous. It makes you necessary."

My throat constricted, her words striking some place tender. I glanced at Calderis, and for once, his expression softened too. "Thank you," I whispered.

Lumira smiled at me. "We're with you, if you need us."

Selvi turned her gaze toward the chamber. "Orielle waits. But time, I fear, does not."

We nodded our farewells and moved onward, deeper into the *Hall of Unspoken Things.*

At the far end of the chamber, beneath a crystalline arch of shifting turquoise, we spotted Orielle. Her form drifted like smoke above the floor, her robes layered in translucent silk, woven with the shimmer of captured breath. Her long, moon-pale hair rippled around her face.

She floated in hushed conversation with Seris, Keeper of Forbidden Love, whose gloved hands cradled a rose carved from starlight. As we approached, Seris offered us a wistful nod, then touched Orielle's heart gently in farewell and drifted away into the whispering mist.

"Orielle," I said quietly.

She turned to face us. Her eyes, a pale opal, were both distant and all-seeing. "Lyra. Calderis. Vex. The current has brought you far tonight."

"We've come to ask about Samuel's unauthorized wish," Calderis said. "We believe it may have triggered the disruption in the seasonal cycle."

Orielle's hair rippled, as if echoing her thoughts. "His voice faded before it was finished, but the echo lingers." She floated down toward the ground, her robes folding around her like petals, and her feet touched the earth with a softness that made no sound.

"Do you know what his wish was?" Calderis asked.

"I do. Because he is dead now, the wish is stuck in the well as you know." The stillness in the chamber deepened. "Like I told your father, Samuel wished to gain access through the portal. He wanted to cross freely into Elarion. Not just observe it, but step through and uncover the truths kept from his world."

"Typical Samuel," Vex grumbled.

"There's something else," Orielle said carefully. "Someone stole a wish echo from my chambers, and someone wished for Samuel to go away forever," Orielle looked at me, and for the first time, something almost sorrowful crossed her expression, "and I know who it was."

"Then tell us," Calderis demanded.

She shook her head, slowly, firmly. "No. The wish was not for death. It was for silence. For absence. A desperate voice, full of hurt. I guard them all, Calderis."

"But that wish might reveal a clue to the killer," Calderis pressed.

"I am not the arbiter," Orielle said gently. "I am the keeper and bound by a code. The moment I choose which voices to reveal, I become something else."

I looked at her, my frustration and understanding warring in equal measure. "Will you help us at all?"

She stepped forward and brushed her fingers across my temple—light and cool like raindrops. "I can give you fragments," she whispered. "Dream threads. Names. Glimpses. Let them come. They will find you in sleep."

I had heard of her Dream Weaving but had never experienced it first-hand. The thought was a little unsettling, but I swallowed, nodding. "Thank you."

As she turned back toward the shifting corridors of whispering memory, I watched her disappear behind filtered light that flickered with all the unsaid things of the world.

"She knows more," I said softly.

"She always does," Calderis said beside me.

And I had the strangest feeling—like someone else was already waiting to speak to me next in a dream...or maybe a nightmare.

THE MORNING LIGHT in Wishville felt too bright for the things I now knew.

Sunbeams streamed through the clouds, casting cheerful glints across the bunting that flapped from streetlamps and storefronts. Everything was still festive on the surface—sugar-dusted pastries in the bakery window, kids chasing ribbon streamers, music tuning up near the bandstand—but underneath it all, the town felt...anxious.

I'd barely made it two steps past the flower stall when Holden spotted me.

"Lyra!" he called, striding across the square with that determined gait that made me want to sprint in the opposite direction.

I pasted on a polite smile and adjusted the strap of my bag. "Morning, Chief."

"You've been hard to track down." He stopped in front of me, his arms crossed over his chest and eyes narrowed beneath that stubborn dark brow. "I swung by your house last night. Your lights were off."

"Oh." I feigned a laugh. "Sorry. I delegate most festival duties, but sometimes I have to personally put out fires that have had me running in ten directions."

Holden didn't look convinced.

"I just," I shrugged, aiming for breezy, "didn't want to drag you into the craziness."

"Since when?" He grunted, then added dryly, "Would've been nice to know you weren't abducted by balloon pirates."

"Next time I'll leave a note," I muttered.

He studied me for a beat longer than necessary, then pulled out his notebook. "Anyway, I've been working things from my end. We questioned Marin Holloway again, and she swears she didn't break into Samuel's place. I'm inclined to believe her, but her alibi is as vague as everyone else's seems to be on the night of the murder."

I nodded, trying to focus.

"And the mayor's on my back," Holden continued. "She wants results. It's day five of WishFest, and the press is starting to circle like seagulls at a fry stand. If we don't make progress soon..."

"I know," I said softly. "The well won't grant a wish until Samuel's murder is resolved." I blinked. *Whoops.*

Holden gave me a sharp look. "You know that the whole wish granting thing is a ruse to keep the tourists coming back, right? You're supposed to be my advisor on this murder case since it's centered around the festival. I need to know you're of sound mind. Please tell me you don't seriously believe the well is magical."

I looked away, pretending to fuss with the strap of my bag again. "I'm just getting into the spirit of the festival, is all."

He sighed, not bothering to hide his frustration. "So-called *magic* aside, if you know something, Lyra—something you're not telling me—"

"I don't," I said quickly, too quickly. "I mean...I *would* tell you if I did."

His jaw tightened, but he let it go. For now. "I'm heading to the station," he said at last. "Keep your phone on. If something shakes loose, I want you there."

"Of course."

He walked off, but I could feel the weight of his doubt and frustration long after he disappeared around the corner. It couldn't be helped. I couldn't reveal everything I had discovered with Calderis in Elarion, for his own good as much as my own.

I didn't go to the booth tents. I didn't check in with the volunteer coordinator or help tie ribbons to the tree in the Square like I was supposed to. Instead, I walked the long way around town, past the edge of the community garden, and through the hedgerow gate behind the row of antique houses.

Samuel's cottage stood quietly under a veil of creeping ivy and wisteria vines, its porch sagging just a little more than I remembered. The door was still sealed with caution tape, but the lock had long since been jimmied by nosy teenagers or restless night owls.

It opened with a soft creak.

Inside, it smelled like dust and paper and faintly of thyme—his favorite herb, apparently, based on the half-empty jars still lining the windowsill. Sunlight filtered in through gauzy curtains, catching the dust motes as they danced lazily across a desk piled with loose sketches, maps, and fragments of old Dweller folklore.

I scanned the room with a different kind of eye this time—not for the obvious, but for the *missing*. For what might have been concealed and not displayed.

Books lined the walls in a kind of organized chaos—one row on politics, another on magical theory, and an entire shelf of Samuel's journals highlighting rumored surface-Dweller relationships across history. One particularly worn spine caught my attention—*Myths of the Hidden Realms*—but when I pulled it, I felt the weight shift oddly.

The cover was real.

The pages were not.

The book had been hollowed out and nestled inside the carved space was a folded piece of parchment, thick with Samuel's sprawling flowery handwriting. It wasn't notes. It was a secret journal entry.

I never meant to fall in love with someone from the world beneath the veil. I knew what it would mean—what it would cost us both—but I couldn't stay away. Her touch was starlight. Her words wildfire.

I would've done anything to cross that threshold and stay. That's why I didn't publish my findings, but it didn't matter. She dumped me when she found out I knew her secret.

She didn't trust me enough to keep it, and my heart is broken.

My throat tightened. Samuel had been involved with a Dweller. He had fallen in love with someone from Elarion. And suddenly, everything else—the memory crystal, the stolen wish token, the broken treaty threads—felt different. Not cold and academic but *personal.*

Emotional.

Dangerous.

I folded the paper gently and slipped it into my bag. I didn't know who his lover was, but I knew this had to stay secret at least for now. As I stepped out into the light, the front porch groaned faintly under my boots. I glanced around, my heart thudding wildly. There was no one in sight.

Still, I couldn't shake the feeling of being watched.

By the time I made it back to the square, Holden was waiting. "Where've you been?" he asked.

I tried to shrug it off. "I was checking in with vendors."

"Funny. You weren't around any of them when I looked."

I blinked. "We must have just missed each other."

Holden didn't respond right away. He looked at me the same way he had when he first took over as the chief of police, like he was cataloguing my every word, tone, and hesitation.

"You seem different," he said. "What's wrong?"

"Nothing. I've just been busy," I replied.

He stared a moment longer, then said, "You know, if you're keeping things from me again because you think I won't understand...you're wrong. I've told you a lot about myself, uncomfortable things about my past, yet I know nearly nothing about you."

I opened my mouth, but nothing came out because I couldn't tell him. My past wasn't just mine...it involved a whole other species.

He shook his head slowly and stepped back, looking hurt. "I hope you remember when everything falls apart—which I'm afraid it will since we're clearly not working together anymore—that I tried to be there for you." Then he turned and walked away.

And I was left alone in the center of a town filled with wishes, secrets, and lies.

The afternoon light in Wishville had that hazy, honeyed quality that made everything feel slower than it was—except for my pulse. My heart was hammering a mile a minute as I ducked around the back of the yarn shop, cutting through alleys.

Vex trotted at my heels, silent and sharp-eyed. "You're making bad decisions," he said under his breath.

"I'm aware," I muttered. "You don't have to make them with me. Go see Fenrin."

"I can't," he grumbled, sounding irritated. "She went back to Elarion."

Which was exactly what I was trying to do. Slipping away during the day was dangerous—risky didn't even cover it—but I couldn't wait until nightfall. Not when the memory of Orielle's words kept whispering through my skull like a haunting melody: *someone stole a wish echo from her chambers, someone wished Samuel would go away for good.*

We reached the well just as a warm breeze drifted through the forest clearing. Its stones gleamed in the afternoon light, deceptively ordinary. Festival music warbled around the tents—accordion notes, laughter, the clink of lemonade glasses. The timing was not ideal. It felt too bright. Too exposed. But no one was making a wish at the moment, so this might be our only chance.

"I don't like this," Vex said.

"I don't either."

I placed a palm against the ancient stones. The hum beneath my skin answered immediately. With one last glance around, I whispered the incantation and stepped over the edge. The veil rose like quicksilver mist, cool and electric, swallowing me whole. Elarion opened around me like a held breath finally released, different every time I passed through.

Today, I landed on moss so soft it felt like memory foam. Trees with crystal-lined branches arched overhead, their leaves glowing in soft, rhythmic pulses of lavender, blue, and rose gold. The air shimmered with a kind of suspended warmth—like twilight caught in amber. Faint birdsong echoed in the distance, though the birds here didn't flap—they drifted, ribbon-like, through the light.

Magic hung in the air like humidity, clinging to my skin, my eyelashes, even the hem of my jacket. I'd had no time to change into my robes and there was no moonlight for cloaking, so I still wore my earthly clothes, but that couldn't be helped.

And then—

Splash.

Behind me.

I whirled around just in time to see something large and very human crash through the veil in a blur of panic and limbs and water.

I gasped. "*No—*"

Holden hit the moss path with a bounce, coughing and soaked to the bone. His dress shirt clung to him like it was trying to escape his suit coat, his blue jeans were heavy with water, and his boots squished as he tried to stand.

"What the—what *is* this—" he gasped, spinning to take in the luminous forest, the floating motes of shimmering pollen, the glowing river that wove between ridged stones like a living ribbon.

He was panicked. Confused. The badge still clipped to his belt glinted in the light like a misplaced artifact. He swiped a hand over the hairs in his beard that kept moving, his gray eyes a bright silver now.

"Intruder!" came a commanding voice.

Drelian.

He burst from the trees like a thunderclap—tall, furious, his staff ignited with swirling violet fire. His eyes blazed aqua green as he saw Holden—clearly human, and definitely not welcome.

"*No!*" I shot out from the glowing ferns and ran between them. "Drelian, don't!"

"Step aside, Guardian," he barked. "He's crossed sacred lines—"

"He didn't know!" I shouted, breathless, my arms wide.

"Wait...what is happening, Lyra?" Holden asked. "I thought you fell into the well. I thought you were going to *drown.*"

"See?" I said desperately. "He tried to save me. It's my fault. The portal hadn't closed yet when he fell in. He didn't mean to breach the veil!"

Holden stared between us, panting, wide-eyed, his hand instinctively brushing his hip where his sidearm rested, but he didn't draw it. He was stunned and clearly trying to stay calm.

"He's armed," Drelian said coldly, raising his staff.

"So are you," I snapped.

Drelian advanced.

And then a voice cut through the air like chilled water. "Stand down."

Calderis.

He stepped from the obsidian arch behind the waterfall, his robes swirling behind him, his expression unreadable. His hair sparkled like frost in moonlight, and the tension in the space shifted the moment he appeared—like the very stones of Elarion recognized him and fell silent.

Drelian froze mid-step.

"That's an order, Drelian," Calderis said calmly, but with a steel that made my spine straighten. "I'll handle this."

"Calderis, he—"

"I said, *stand down*."

"Tread carefully, my friend." Drelian clenched his jaw hard enough I could hear it click. "Vaerion won't like this."

"He won't know about it," Calderis said, looking us each in the eye, "because none of us will speak of it."

A long pause passed before Drelian gave a stiff nod and disappeared into the trees like a vanishing flame.

Then Calderis turned to me, his gaze sharper than any knife. "Did anyone else see him follow you?"

"No," I said, my heart still thundering. "At least, I don't think so. No one was near the well when I came through."

He gave a short nod then turned his attention to Holden, who still hadn't moved except to wipe dripping water out of his eyes.

"Is someone going to explain what just happened?" Holden asked. "Because I just watched you throw yourself into the well, and yet somehow, you're not dead...not even close. What is all of this?"

I stepped toward him carefully with my hands open. "You weren't supposed to follow me."

"Sorry," he said tightly. "Next time I'll *ignore* my gut instinct and let you drown."

"Holden—"

"I knew you were keeping things from me," he said, still gaping at his surroundings. "What is this place?"

"This is Elarion," I said. "It's a hidden realm. The one from the legend and folklore tales. A world beneath Wishville—ancient, magical, alive."

He blinked, looking past me to the trees glowing faintly like stained glass. "This isn't just...some underground cave system. This is *real*."

"Yes."

His eyes locked onto mine on the verge of panic. "And you? You've been coming here this whole time?"

I nodded slowly. "Because I belong to both worlds."

"What does that mean?"

"It means..." I took a breath, then said it out loud. "I'm half-Dweller. My mother was from Elarion. My father was human."

His gaze widened and lips parted.

"I was briefly raised in Wishville until my father died, then I spent most of my life in Elarion with my mother. When she later vanished, the well chose me to take her place, so I rose to the surface once more."

"Chose you for what?"

"To guard the treaty, keep the peace, and protect the balance between our worlds. That's why I've been so insistent on keeping WishFest going. If a human's wish isn't granted once per season, then the treaty will break, the portal will open, and war will likely resume. I'm the Guardian of the Well."

"This is all too much." Holden let out a shaky breath, rubbing a hand down his soaked face. "You lied to me."

"I didn't lie. I hid it."

He laughed once—bitter, short. "That's just a lie with more steps."

"I was trying to protect people just like you, but in both our worlds. If this world gets exposed—"

"People like me wouldn't understand," he said, his voice angry.

"No," I countered. "Greedy people like scientists and fanatics." My tone softened. "You? I hoped you might."

The air between us vibrated, but not with magic this time...with emotion.

Calderis stepped forward, reminding me he was still there. "He can't return without a memory seal."

"A memory what?" Holden looked between the two of us, his hand sliding near his holster once more.

"He's my ally, Calderis. I need him. You know that."

"Lyra—"

"I insist," I said firmly. "He's not leaving yet. Not until he hears everything."

Holden crossed his arms. "I'm not going anywhere until I get some answers."

I looked at him—really looked at him. His soaked shirt. The tension in his jaw. The betrayal in his eyes...and underneath it, something else. Curiosity?

"Then come," I said. "Let me show you the truth." Because the well had chosen me, but now I needed to choose who I trusted to stand beside me.

CHAPTER
Sixteen

CALDERIS'S FURY was quieter now, but no less dangerous. It simmered beneath his words like molten silver beneath ice, waiting to erupt. "I'll go to the Council," he said tightly, pacing a few feet from us beneath the shimmer-leaf canopy. The trees above swayed without wind. "No one saw you enter the well except Drelian. He'll keep your silence, and I'll keep the Council distracted."

The ground beneath us was soft and spongy, the stones edged in glowing lichen. Today, the air smelled of sun-warmed herbs—ancient and clean. It should have felt like a sanctuary, but the heat in Calderis's voice said otherwise.

"I'll cover for him," he went on, flicking his gaze toward Holden with distaste, "but only this once. Be quick, Lyra. If my father finds out a human crossed the veil, he'll demand blood."

"I didn't mean to fall through your magic portal," Holden grumbled. "Maybe next time put up a *sign*."

"Next time," Calderis said icily, standing a good six inches above Holden's six-foot-four frame, "you may not get out alive."

Before Holden could fire back, Calderis conjured glittering midnight-blue robes—woven through with silver runes and trailing with faint magical threads that curled like wisps of breath in cold air.

"Wear these," he instructed. "They'll mask your origin enough, at least, to fool anyone who glances too quickly, but don't speak. Don't hesitate. And *do not* draw attention." As he handed me mine, his hand lingered just long enough for me to feel the edge of betrayal beneath his control. Then he was gone—vanishing into the carved stone archway in a burst of starlight.

We dressed in silence under the camouflaging branches of a tree. My robe fit like a second skin, the fabric impossibly light and yet protective, so different from my own robes but nice. It felt alive against my fingertips, like it recognized me, and I realized it was my mother's. He must have gotten it from her chambers, left untouched since she'd vanished. When I stayed in Elarion, that's where I lived.

Holden, soaked and muttering under his breath, struggled to lace his collar until I stepped in and helped, tying the small loop near his throat with quiet efficiency. His skin was warm beneath the fabric, but his eyes were unreadable.

When we were cloaked with our hoods up, we looked less like invaders and more like traveling scholars on a silent vow—an old and believable cover in Elarion. I doubted it would fool anyone *truly* paying attention, but for now, it would do.

Holden looked at me sharply. "So let me get this straight. You're a half magical being, guardian of Wishville's well, and in charge of keeping an ancient inter-realm treaty intact?"

I winced. "In so many words, yes."

He studied me curiously. "How old are you?"

I squirmed under his intense stare, then thrust my chin up. "Older than you, and that's all I'm going to say about that."

He let out a long breath, rubbing the hood over his drying hair. "And all this time, you let me chase theories and suspects, while you already had access to the truth."

"I don't know the truth," I said. "Not all of it. I'm still piecing it together."

"But you know more than me," he replied, "and you kept that to yourself."

His words landed like weighted stones.

"I wasn't trying to shut you out," I said softly. "I was trying to protect both our worlds."

He said nothing, his mouth a thin line now.

We walked in tense silence through the woods.

The paths here twisted in gentle spirals, laid with quartz veins and dotted with glowing mushrooms. The air shimmered with floating globes that looked like fireflies suspended in amber. Birds called out overhead—no caws or chirps, but long musical notes like flutes carved from wind.

We were just crossing a ridge when a sound broke the stillness: a soft, brittle sob. I froze. Holden followed my gaze, and together we stepped off the path and followed the sound through a break in the foliage.

Beyond the trees, the Lirien River curved through a meadow lit by twilight bioluminescence. The water flowed like liquid crystal—smooth, silent, glowing faintly blue. Flowers dotted the banks—delicate things with wide silver petals and stems that expanded and contracted with light like breath.

Kneeling at the edge of the river was Seris.

She wore a gown of layered white and pearl, and it spilled around her like water frozen mid-motion. Her hair fell loose, tangled in the reeds, and in her hands she held a small silver charm that glittered—shaped like a broken star.

She didn't turn when we approached. "I know you're there," she said, her voice soft and watery. "Only Orielle walks without sound."

I stepped closer. "We need to talk." As a half-blood of both worlds, Dual Sight allowed me to perceive both surface illusions and subterranean truths.

She looked up. Her eyes were glassy, her lashes wet. She looked beautiful in the way broken things are—delicate yet still dangerous. "Then speak."

"It's about Samuel," I said gently.

Her lips trembled. She looked down at the charm again. "You've found something."

"We know," I said. She was the keeper of forbidden love, including her own. "You loved him."

Holden looked at me with a raised brow.

A sharp inhale caught in her throat, drawing our gazes as a single tear dropped into the river. "I did," she whispered. "More than I meant to."

Holden crossed his arms. "So, why'd you sabotage him? You hacked his profile and matched him with Evelyn Poe to push him away, didn't you."

My gaze shot to his, realizing he was bluffing with a guess.

Seris didn't deny it. "I was afraid," she whispered. "Afraid he'd expose me, and that I would lose everything. So, I did what cowards do. I manipulated fate and hoped it would save us both."

"It didn't," I said.

"No," she whispered. "He loved me anyway, even when I tried to vanish from his life."

"Your wish archive was sealed after his death," I said. "Why?"

She looked at us. "Because I'm the one who made the wish."

My heart skipped a beat. "The wish that he'd go away?"

"I didn't wish him dead," she said quickly, fiercely. "I just wanted him gone, quiet...erased from the ache in my heart. I thought if I could just wish him out of my world, I could go back to being who I was before."

"And the wish echo?"

"It was one of his wishes. I stole it," she whispered. "I needed a piece of him. Orielle found out...and she covered for me."

"Because you're friends," I said.

She nodded.

"Why didn't you tell anyone?" Holden asked.

"Because the heart is the most dangerous relic of all," she whispered.

Silence fell like snow.

Seris stood, her robes trailing wet behind her. "If I could take it back, I would, but wishes are irreversible. That's the rule even for us." And then she turned and walked into the trees, her figure dissolving into mist and light.

Holden watched her go then looked at me. "So, the one who loved him most is the one who pushed him away, and now he's dead. What cruel irony." He shook his head. "That's messed up."

I swallowed the lump in my throat. "Wishes have power."

He looked at me. "So do secrets."

And for the first time, I wondered which one would destroy us first.

I knew we didn't have much time left before we risked being caught. I had promised Calderis I would hurry, but there was one more thing I needed to check out.

The deeper we moved into the sealed corridors, the heavier the air became.

It wasn't oppressive exactly, more reverent. Like even the dust here knew better than to stir. Light filtered down from the arched ceiling in threads of blue and silver, refracted through crystal inlays carved into the stone. Faint whispers brushed the edges of my thoughts like a memory sighing.

Holden walked beside me, his borrowed robe brushing against the polished onyx floor. His face was drawn, shadowed in the blue light, his mouth a thin line of quiet suspicion and wonder. "Let me guess," he said under his breath, "this place is off-limits for a reason."

"Very," I whispered. "It's called the *Heart Chamber*. It houses love stories that broke laws. Bonds that nearly unraveled the treaty. Magic made from longing and memory."

He glanced sideways at me. "So basically, the most dangerous kind of magic."

"Yes," I said softly. "The kind that's made when someone

chooses love over everything else." Vaerion had said I would have access to all archives for my investigation.

This was the moment of truth.

The door was carved with a great rose of flame—its petals layered in burnished gold and soft red. I placed my hand at the center. The sigil recognized my touch instantly, threads of heat uncoiling into my palm. A gentle warmth—not burning, but intimate—spread up my arm.

The rose unraveled, petal by petal, until the door dissolved.

We stepped into the vault.

It was stunning.

The chamber rose in a smooth dome of pale stone veined with glowing lavender light. Hovering relics—memory crystals, pressed tokens, enchanted keepsakes—floated like stars in soft orbits around carved pedestals. Each one flickered gently with its own light and magic. They hummed. They sang. Some pulsed slow and sad like the remnants of lullabies. Others glowed fierce and red, restless in their eternal ache. The air smelled like candlewax and aged parchment, with an undertone of something softer—rosewater, maybe, or jasmine tea.

Holden took a step inside, his voice hushed. "This place...it's alive."

"Not alive," I said, my voice catching, "but still breathing."

A crystal near the center drew me in—a teardrop shape, edged in gold filigree. It glowed with a soft, wounded pink.

"Seris and Samuel," I whispered.

The moment my fingers brushed the edge, the crystal flared, and the memory unfolded.

Samuel's voice, young and unguarded, laughed in the air like a ripple on still water. "You're not real," he said to someone offscreen. "You can't be."

Seris's voice, low and aching, replied, "And yet you keep finding me."

Their story bloomed in Wishville: She'd found an opening in the Whisper Woods and slipped to the surface out of curiosity even though it was forbidden. She met Samuel and fell in love, continuing with quiet meetings beside mountain streams, a stolen kiss under glowing lamplights, and secret notes hidden in library books as she grew bolder. Each fragment floated by like petals caught in a slow wind, but then the laughter faded. The memory began to flicker as the truth of who Seris was and where she came from emerged. He became obsessed, demanding to know more about her world.

Seris's face turned away, her lips trembling.

Samuel reached for her—and missed.

"Don't," she whispered. "If you touch me, I won't leave."

He managed to pick her pocket before she slipped away, holding the memory crystal as the last piece of her.

And the vision collapsed into silence.

I stepped away.

Holden didn't say a word.

He followed me to the next crystal. This one hovered lower, closer to the ground, shaped like a flame frozen mid-dance. I reached out. Samuel again—only this time, his voice was ragged.

"Portal...truth...too late..."

The image was fractured—Samuel clutching a journal, his hands trembling, standing before something we couldn't quite see. A glow spilled around him—cold, blue, unnatural—and then darkness.

The crystal dimmed.

My breath caught. "That was his final memory," I said.

"Not a wish," Holden murmured, "a warning."

I looked at him, and for the first time, I saw the fear in his eyes. The way he was piecing things together and watching the picture twist.

He shook his head slowly. "I don't know what to believe anymore."

I opened my mouth to answer but then stopped. The chamber seemed to shift around us, beckoning me toward one more relic. This one was nestled in the crook of a silver tree whose leaves were made of crystal flowers. A memory crystal shaped like a curved shell glowed there, pale as moonlight. I knew it before I touched it.

"My mother," I breathed. I didn't wait. I reached forward, and the vision bloomed around us.

A woman stood barefoot in a field of fire flowers...Elarion meadows. Her hair gleamed silver in the sun. She laughed—my laugh—and turned toward a tall man in a faded brown coat. He was human. Dark curls, warm smile, ink-stained hands.

"You shouldn't be here," she said softly. "The treaty forbids it."

"You belong to me just as I belong to you no matter where we are," he replied.

They met in the middle of the flowers, and the world seemed to go quiet.

"We can't exist in each other's worlds, but she can. She will straddle both our worlds," my mother whispered, dropping her hands over her stomach. "Let her choose where her heart belongs, before they choose for her."

The crystal dimmed, and I stepped back.

Holden looked at me, his brow furrowed, something soft and shaken in his expression. "That was your father?"

I nodded. "He gave up everything to protect her. She gave up everything to love him. And I...I came from that. From something that was never meant to be allowed. I owe it to them to fight for both worlds."

I turned from the tree and walked to the center of the chamber, my heart pounding.

"I grew up feeling like a fracture," I said, my voice raw now. "Like I didn't belong on the surface, and I wasn't welcome here. My father died when I was little, and my mother disappeared when I was barely an adult. Vanished. The elders never told me why. I didn't ask because I didn't want to think that she willingly left me. So, I kept quiet. I kept to myself. I studied, I listened, and I never let anyone close enough to find the crack in me."

Holden stepped forward, looking strong and handsome and safe.

"And then the well chose me to take my mother's place as the guardian. It's only recently I've come to suspect my mother didn't leave on her own. I think something happened to her, and I'm not going to stop looking until I figure out what." The light caught the edges of the flame-crystal behind us, casting fire across the floor. "I didn't choose to be the guardian," I whispered, "but I did choose to carry the burden alone."

Holden reached out slowly, his hand brushing my sleeve. "You might have had to at one time," he said softly, lacing his fingers with mine, "but you don't now."

The air between us vibrated—charged, tender, uncertain.

"I didn't know if I could trust you," I admitted, holding on tight.

"And now?"

I looked up into his eyes. They were stormy and conflicted, but open.

"Now I want to," I said, "even if it terrifies me." I took a shaky breath. "If I get close to you, I will ultimately lose you like I did my father."

He didn't pull away, holding me captive with his gaze. "Lose me how?"

"Like I said...I'm older." I let go of his hand as the truth reminded me to be wary with my heart. "You will never grow to be my age."

"My father always taught me age is just a number," he said softly, and after a beat added, "and from my experience, I've learned that no one ever truly knows how much time they have. Best enjoy life and live for the moment."

We stood there in the hush of the *Heart Chamber*, surrounded by centuries of forbidden love and flickering memories, and for the first time, I didn't feel like an intruder in either world.

I felt seen.

CHAPTER
Seventeen

EVENING HAD SETTLED over Wishville like a velvet curtain, and the well settled behind us, its shimmer fading and magic hidden beneath the water. We had ditched the robes Calderis had given us in the bushes of Elarion before we'd crossed through the portal back to Wishville before Calderis could insist on a memory seal again. I couldn't let that happen. Holden stood beside me, his hair still damp and face lit in amber hues from the lampposts overhead.

We were halfway out of the grove when a sound stopped us cold.

"Well, bless my bramble biscuits—did you *see* that?" Belle's voice rang out, laced with awe and mischief.

Holden and I turned slowly. All three Wellies were staring at us like they'd just seen unicorns hop out of a washing machine.

Belle clutched her oversized root beer float like a chalice. Tilly had a miniature dreamcatcher dangling from her belt, currently spinning in wild, erratic circles. Dot was already whispering into her teacup, her eyebrows climbing higher with every imagined syllable.

"It looked like they *crawled* out of the well," Tilly whispered, shielding her mouth like it helped. "Just *appeared*. Pop! Like sprouts."

Holden coughed. "Evening, ladies. Nothing magical happening here. Just, uh—routine inspection."

I added quickly, "Low water levels. We're just keeping an eye on the groundwater flow. With the weather being unpredictable and all..."

Dot squinted at me from behind her massive glasses. "Since when do groundwater inspections shimmer?"

Belle sniffed. "You're both glowing like you rolled in fairy pollen. Especially him. That's not normal."

"Detergent," Holden said blandly, brushing his sleeve. "Experimental."

Tilly leaned in. "Are you part-Dryad? Or Sylph? Because if so, I *need* to know. My spleen journal is very particular about elemental proximity."

"Gotta go!" I chirped, grabbing Holden's arm and steering us into the crowd. "Enjoy your floats!"

They called after us—Belle asking if we'd "met any star beasts," Dot claiming she *felt* a ripple—but the festival swallowed us before they could catch up.

WishFest was busier than ever, both in the clearing by the well and down the path into the town square. String lights stretched across the square like glowing spiderwebs, crisscrossing overhead in arcs. Booths lined the cobblestone paths—offering maple fudge, charm bottles, and petting zoo miniature goat stuffed animals with sparkly horns hot-glued to their heads. The air pulsed with fiddle music from the gazebo and smelled like roasted almonds, mulled cider, and a faint trace of campfire.

It should've felt festive, but I couldn't shake the tension under my skin.

"Think they bought it?" Holden asked, tugging on his wrinkled suit coat.

"Hard to say," I murmured. "Tilly once claimed a squirrel was her reincarnated grandmother and nobody blinked. So...maybe."

We passed Eli hanging a row of lanterns carved like moons, each one bobbing gently in the breeze. Children ran beneath them with glowing wands, shouting spells of their own invention, pretending they had magic. Trip directed people using his flashlight and blowing his whistle. People laughed and danced, but at the edge of it all—just beyond the cider tent—I spotted a conversation that didn't belong.

Holden saw it too. He touched my arm. "Over there."

Mayor Hemsworth, regal in her candy apple red peacoat and festival brooch, stood in hushed conversation with Henry McAlister. He was hunched slightly, one hand curled into a fist at his side, his gaze darting around like he expected to be watched. The mayor's jaw was tight, her eyes shaded with something colder than concern. She kept her hands folded, but her stance was unmistakably assertive.

A deal.

A warning.

A quiet threat, perhaps.

"What is he doing?" I whispered. "No one remembered him at the zoning hearings. Now he's whispering with the mayor?"

Holden narrowed his eyes. "He did say she was interested in his redevelopment project."

"That's true, and she admitted she was looking for different streams of revenue, but now you understand why we can't reduce the number of festivals. So much is at stake if the treaty is broken."

He nodded. "The festivals might increase crime, but I'll take that over war any day. I was deployed twice when I was a marine." His face darkened. "It's not something I ever want to experience again."

Before we could move to do anything, a crash tore through the square—sharp, metallic, and loud.

"Back off, you snake-oil peddler!" Reed Callahan's voice boomed. He shoved Stan McDuff into a storefront strung with wind chimes, sending the delicate metal spiraling through the air in a shrieking chorus of doom.

Festivalgoers screamed.

A toddler wailed.

A pie went airborne and landed in someone's hood.

"You've been poking around my workshop!" Reed shouted, his hair wild, his shirt half-unbuttoned. "You're trying to sabotage my invention!"

"Your invention nearly *imploded* the east glen!" Stan barked back. "We're lucky no one fell into your experimental crater!"

Holden was already moving. He pushed through the crowd with the speed of someone used to dealing with drunks and brawlers—and idiots with tempers. *"Hey!"* he shouted, shoving between them. "This is a *public* event, not your personal grudge match."

Reed's face was flushed, his breath coming hard. "He's a coward who can't stand progress! He stole my invention."

Stan pointed a finger. "I did no such thing. He's a reckless lunatic experimenting with nature! He's going to ruin our town."

"Cool it," Holden barked. "Both of you, *now*." He stepped between them, one hand outstretched, the other near his badge. His presence grounded people when things tipped too far toward danger.

Reed exhaled, his shoulders slumping. Stan muttered something under his breath and stalked off, carrying a bag of bottles and cans. I joined Holden just as the crowd began murmuring again, hungry for the next piece of gossip.

"I swear..." He dragged a hand down his face. "One more outburst and I'm going to start handing out fines and anger management pamphlets."

I smiled faintly. "Do you think Stan stole the prototype?"

"Maybe. People do crazy things when they're scared," he said. "A man was murdered, and a random crater with an unusual pattern burned into it leave people in a fight or flight mode, looking for someone to blame."

My gaze drifted toward the mayor and Henry, who had already slipped away. "Well, I'm not about to run. It's time we stood our ground and fought for the festival. I've got a sneaking suspicion our *someone to blame* just left."

"That's what I'm here for." He nodded once, following my gaze. "What do you have in mind?"

"Let me think on it. There has to be something we can do."

That night, I fell asleep with questions still gnawing at me like mice in the walls.

Why was Mayor Hemsworth talking to Henry McAlister in secret? What kind of hold did he have on her? And what were they planning behind the scenes while the town lost itself in savory crepes and lantern parades? Sleep took me slowly, dragging me under in waves of color and candlelight.

And then—the air shifted.

I found myself in a dreamworld painted in shades of silver and dusk-blue, the edges rippling like fabric caught in a slow breeze. I stood in a vast hall of glass trees, their trunks clear as crystal, their branches hung with ribbons of sound. Soft whispers floated through the canopy—lost voices, old wishes, secrets too fragile to be spoken aloud.

"Orielle," I breathed.

She appeared like a reflection stepping forward from still water, her robes trailing behind her in streams of pearl-gray mist. Her hair drifted like a waterfall, and her eyes—unreadable pools of moonlight—met mine with quiet urgency.

"Whispers find their way to me," she said softly, "even the ones buried in silence."

I nodded. "You came because something's wrong."

"Yes." She tilted her head. "The surface world spins toward shadow. Not because of magic...but because of greed."

A chill crept over my skin. "You're talking about the mayor."

Orielle didn't confirm it directly. She never did. Her words were always riddles wrapped in reverence.

"There is a hand that signs decrees and a heart that hides debts," she said. "Someone you trust is not who they pretend to be."

I swallowed. "Henry?"

"No," she said quietly. "He is many things—calculating, bitter—but not the one who spun the first lie. He merely saw the unraveling and stitched himself a way in."

The crystal trees hummed softly around us. In the branches above, a ribbon of sound twisted low—three voices speaking in fragments:

"She promised me—"

"It's all gone..."

"—They'll find out."

I looked up. "Where do I start?"

Orielle raised her hand, and the dream shifted again.

We stood now in the mayor's office—only it wasn't solid. It flickered like a memory half-remembered. Her desk was littered with papers, the edge of a bank statement visible beneath a file stamped **CONFIDEN-TIAL**. *A torn envelope peeked out of a drawer. A single coin spun slowly on the polished wood surface—faster, faster, until it vanished in a puff of smoke.*

"There is a ledger where there should be light," Orielle said. "A record hidden in plain sight. Look where she keeps what she doesn't want counted."

"A financial trail," I murmured. "Hidden funds?"

"Debt dressed in civic pride," she said. "Shame turned into cement."

The dream quivered again.

Now we stood at the edge of the well—only it was paved over, hollowed out and replaced with a gleaming marble replica turned into a fountain crowned with gaudy lights and water spewing out the top of the well. **The Wishing Well Wonderland Theme Park**, *someone had scrawled in stylized lettering. A banner above read:* **Coming Soon – Brought to You by McAlister Redevelopment Group**.

I turned to Orielle, a sick feeling curling in my gut. "They want to destroy it."

She nodded once.

"But if I accuse her without proof—"

"Then look deeper," Orielle said. "Find the clue she left behind. The town sees only her ribbon-cuttings and confident smiles. But in quiet corners, paper bleeds the truth."

"I need to get into her office."

She stepped closer, and her voice dropped. "And remember, Lyra...not every villain wears a mask. And not every monster is born from magic."

The dream began to fade.

I tried to hold on, reaching out. "Wait. One more thing—"

Her voice came as an echo, layered with wind and bell chimes. "Trust your instinct. But trust your doubts more."

Then everything dissolved into gray light.

I woke with the dawn pressing through my window, the sound of birdsong filtered through the rustling leaves of the forest outside.

Vex stirred at my side, blinking at me with narrowed suspicion, as if he'd just returned from some secret errand of his own.

I sat up slowly, the dream lingering sharp and clear.

Orielle hadn't shown me everything—but she'd given me enough. There was a paper trail, somewhere. A ledger. A record. And if I could find it, I could stop whatever the mayor and Henry were planning before it was too late. I didn't need to expose magic to fight corruption. I just needed the truth.

Save the well, solve Samuel's murder, and restore the treaty in forty-eight hours...

No pressure.

I slipped through the alley behind *Town Hall* just as the sun breached the edge of the trees, its morning light turning the dew into diamonds on the grass. The town was still asleep or at least pretending to be. The booths from WishFest sat half-covered in tarps. Streamers fluttered like tired sighs.

Even the wind held its breath.

Beside me, Vex padded silently, his tail flicking with the kind of focus only a half-Whispen feline could manage. His fur shimmered faintly in the low light, a glimmer of his true form tucked neatly beneath midnight black silk.

"Okay," I whispered, pausing beneath the emergency stairwell. "I know this is risky, but Orielle said the proof was in her office, something she didn't want counted. If we find the ledger or those bank statements—anything to prove what she's been hiding—we can stop Henry's project before it breaks the treaty."

Vex let out a low, vibrating hum, like a cat with a thundercloud in its chest. His eyes glowed faintly—pale green today, rimmed with starlight.

"Don't give me that look," I grumbled. "I'm not telling Holden until I have something solid. You know how he gets. He'll want to file a form just to suspect her."

He'd also want backup, Vex thought dryly, his voice a smooth, smoky purr in my mind, *and a flashlight, and possibly a council-approved permit.*

I snorted under my breath. "Exactly."

The side door lock yielded easily to the enchanted key I kept hidden in my boot cuff—one that opened any door, and one I only used in emergencies.

This counted.

We crept inside.

Town Hall smelled like lemon floor polish. The overhead fluorescents remained off, but dawn's light slipped in through the blinds in thin slices. It made everything look a little like an old polaroid—grainy, delicate, already fading.

We passed the council meeting room, its vinyl-padded chairs lined up in perfect rows like obedient citizens.

Vex's ears twitched as we moved past. *I've always hated this place,* he muttered in my brain. *Too many rules. Too much beige.*

We reached the mayor's office at the end of the corridor. I glanced around, then whispered, "Let me do the talking if we get caught. You just pretend to be a normal, morally supportive cat."

Vex flicked an ear and gave me a look that could sour milk. *My moral support is conditional on not getting caught.*

Inside, the office was decorated with framed diplomas, fake hydrangeas, and a bookshelf organized by spine color. Everything screamed, *Look how trustworthy I am.* But the room itself gave off a vibe of hiding something under its too-perfect surface.

I crossed to the desk, kneeling beside it. Drawer by drawer, I worked my way through paperclips, sealed envelopes, and a stress ball shaped like a gavel. But the bottom drawer was locked.

I slid my enchanted key into the lock. It clicked open with a sound far too loud in the hush. Inside was a slim black binder with a cracked spine. The tab read:

Historical Festival Budget—Confidential

Bingo.

I flipped it open...and felt my stomach drop.

Page after page of falsified entries, ghost expenses, and siphoned funds marked under vague headers like "infrastructure consulting" and "festival overhead variance." But it was the wire transfer at the back that turned my blood to ice.

Debt Repayment – Sable Mark Casino Group

Vex nosed the page, his eyes narrowing. *She used the town's money to pay off a gambling debt.*

I swallowed hard. "She didn't just mismanage the budget...she stole from it. And Henry's involved. Look. These payments are routed through his shell company. He's been blackmailing her to greenlight the redevelopment project."

Which would dismantle the treaty grounds and expose the portal.

"Exactly." I stood slowly with the binder in my hands. "She betrayed the entire town to cover her losses, and Henry's using it to build his amusement park monstrosity."

Vex arched his back, the tip of his tail twitching. *If you ever let someone put a churro cart next to the sacred spring, I'm defecting to Elarion permanently.*

I was about to respond when the sound of boots echoed sharply down the hallway.

I whirled, clutching the binder just as Holden stepped into view, his expression hard and unreadable.

His gaze dropped to the open drawer, then to the binder in my hands, and finally to my partner-in-crime.

Vex blinked slowly and very deliberately said, "Surprise."

Holden stared at him for a full three seconds. "The *cat* talks?"

Vex yawned. "The cop finally notices."

Holden shook his head, clearly not able to process everything at once, and turned his attention to me. "How long have you been breaking into government offices?"

I opened my mouth, and then closed it.

Vex, the traitor, sauntered over and leaped onto the mayor's desk, settling himself primly on top of the evidence.

"Wait," Holden said slowly, frowning. "Did your cat just *glow*?"

Vex blinked, and then promptly vanished into mist.

Holden recoiled. "What the—Lyra. Your *cat* just did a smoke bomb vanish."

"He's magical, too. Half-cat half-Whispen."

"Half what-in?"

"I'll explain later." I shoved the ledger into Holden's hands. "Read this first."

Giving up, he skimmed the pages, and his expression darkened with each one. "She embezzled from the festival fund to pay loan sharks," he murmured. "And now she's selling us out to cover the rest."

A heel clicked down the hallway.

The front door slammed.

We froze.

Mayor Hemsworth appeared in the doorway moments later, her keys jangling in one hand and coffee in the other...until she saw us. Her face blanched.

"Good morning, Mayor," Holden said coolly, flipping the

ledger open to a very incriminating page. "Care to explain why the festival fund is missing half its budget and being funneled through an LLC tied to Henry McAlister?"

She dropped the keys, and her coffee hit the floor with a ceramic crash. "I—I don't know what you're talking about."

"Oh, I think you do," he said. "I also think it's time we had a very public meeting." He stepped forward and pulled the cuffs from his belt. "Mayor Eliza Hemsworth, you're under arrest for embezzlement, conspiracy to defraud the town of Wishville, and misuse of public funds."

Her lips trembled. "You don't understand. If I didn't pay them, they were going to—"

Holden held up a hand. "You can explain it to the judge, and the townspeople whose money you stole."

As he read her rights, Vex reappeared on the window ledge, his tail flicking smugly. I met his gaze and gave a subtle nod. The game had changed. The magic wasn't the only thing we had to protect. Sometimes, the real danger came from the people who claimed to believe in wishes—while quietly trying to sell them out.

CHAPTER

Eighteen

HOLDEN'S CRUISER pulled away from *Town Hall* with the mayor in the backseat, its blue-and-white lights fading in the distance. The silence that followed felt weighted, like a storm crouching low on the horizon.

"Well," I muttered, watching the taillights vanish, "that's one snake down."

"Plenty more in the grass," Vex said, his voice low and velvety, edged in something older than time. He stretched, his silvery fur rippling. "Henry still slithers freely, and I don't trust a man who starches his collar on a Saturday."

I snorted. "Come on. Let's find out what else he's hiding on his 'Wishing Well Wonderland,' though I'm not sure it will go through now that he's been exposed."

Vex trotted beside me. "Even the name offends me," he muttered. "It sounds like something a bad Santa would pitch."

Henry McAlister had a smaller office in town compared to the one at his construction company sight. This one was tucked inside a sad beige box of a building—formerly a bingo hall, now repurposed into what he optimistically called "a boutique planning headquarters." It smelled like old glue and expired ambition.

I eyed the door. "Can you—"

Vex rolled his eyes, his pupils slitting. "Honestly, what would you do without me?" A faint shimmer passed through his paw as he tapped the lock.

Click.

"I would have used my enchanted key," I clarified, pushing the door open, "but you were closer."

Inside was chaos disguised as corporate professionalism. Blueprints were splayed across every surface. A stack of glossy folders towered dangerously beside a coffee cup that had fossilized into sludge. But front and center, gleaming like a snake shedding its skin, sat a branded portfolio:

The Wishing Well Wonderland—A Magical Adventure Destination.

Vex leaped onto the desk and sniffed. "This smells like sugar, lies, and bankruptcy."

I opened the folder and instantly felt ill. "There's a food court shaped like a clover field," I said, flipping past artist renderings of costumed mascots and overpriced gift shops. Then I sucked in a breath. "A 'Portal Plunge' ride. No one's supposed to know there's a portal. And—oh gods—Whispen plushies that squeal 'Make a Wish!' when you squeeze them."

Vex growled. "If I see a child waving one of those with ketchup fingers, I will combust."

Tucked at the back was a page marked "Permit Strategy." I scanned it, my breath hitching. "This is a forged Historical Society approval. It's backdated, stamped, and signed. Clearly, it's a fake."

Vex dug into a cabinet and pulled out a binder labeled "Outreach." Inside were clearly bribes: honorariums, 'generous donations,' sponsorships. One page even listed 'Anticipated Obstructionists' with suggested 'Incentives.'

"Is that a hit list?" I asked, horrified.

Vex sniffed. "More like a party invitation to a blackmail buffet dinner."

My hands curled around the folder. "We need to burn this down. Not literally," I added as Vex's ears twitched. "We take this to Marin and have her print it. The truth will have the town in an uproar. This goes way beyond bribing the mayor." We left the office and headed to our next destination.

The Wish Weekly's front window was crammed with overlapping flyers, festival posters, and half-laminated headlines.

Vex eyed a spinning rack of brochures with contempt. "I'll never understand why humans need to name their drama," he hissed. "News. Newsflash. Headlines. In our world, we just call it 'regret.'"

Before we reached the door, a figure slipped in from the side alley—hood low, back hunched, sneakers too clean.

Rowan Baxter.

He turned just long enough to catch sight of us before ducking into the morning fog.

Vex's fur bristled. "The whisper-sneaker returns."

I squinted. "What is he up to now?"

Inside, Marin Holloway was scowling as if she'd just smelled something rotten. She glanced up from her cluttered desk. "Lyra. You just missed your little spy."

"Rowan?"

"He said he had a tip. Something about Samuel. I stepped out to get coffee, and he started rifling through my drawer like it owed him rent."

Vex hopped up onto her desk, his voice whispering through my mind, *That man smells like mildew and guilt.*

I handed her the folder. "Forget him. This is the real story. Henry McAlister's plan for the well—theme parks, fake permits, bribery. And he had the mayor helping him."

Marin opened the packet and let out a whistle. "Oh, my lord. He was going to turn the well into *The Wishing Well Wonderland.*"

"And pave over sacred ground in the process," I added. "This isn't redevelopment. It's desecration with branding."

She flipped faster now, her eyes wide. "These signatures are forged. These donation charts are criminal."

Vex stretched, his tail flicking against a stapler as he spoke through my mind once more. *If you include the plushies, it also qualifies as a crime against taste.*

Marin looked up. Did your cat just say something? I swear his meows sound like words sometimes. She shrugged that off and refocused. "If I run this story, it's going to blow up the entire festival. Maybe the town board, too."

I met her gaze. "Do it."

She hesitated. "You sure you're ready for that kind of fallout?"

I nodded. "It's the only way to stop him."

"Then consider it done. It'll be out in a couple hours."

By midafternoon, Wishville had officially combusted.

Marin's headline had hit every mailbox, café counter, and library bulletin board:

WISHING WELL WONDERLAND: THE SECRET SCHEME TO SELL OUR SOULS (AND OUR SACRED SITE)

Subhead: **Mayor Hemsworth Arrested in Alleged Embezzlement and Development Scandal.**

The effect was instant.

Crowds gathered at the square like bees around a lightning-struck hive. People waved copies of *The Wish Weekly* like protest banners, their voices rising in stunned disbelief and righteous anger.

"They were going to put a food court in place of our stage on the festival grounds?" Betsy Plum barked, her apron dusted with flour as she leaned out *The Twisted Loaf's* front door. "Over my dead sourdough!"

"I *knew* it," Fiona Fitzwhistle said from the curb in front of her *Once Upon a Time* bookstore, folding her arms across her gingham blazer. "The mayor's been acting as squirrely as a raccoon on espresso. And Henry McAlister? He gave off corporate creep long before this."

Across the street, the Wellies had gathered in full regalia. Dot wore a polka dot cape. Tilly carried her trusty spleen journal and a crystal wand. Belle wore a tiara she insisted had been humming since sunrise.

"This is exactly what I predicted." Belle thrust the tiara forward like a divining rod. "The well is offended. You *do not* slap animatronics on a sacred vortex!"

"They wanted to turn our beloved wishing well into a popcorn stand," Dot muttered darkly. "I should've hexed him when I had the chance."

Tilly nodded grimly. "I *knew* that man smelled like doom, and the mayor always wears evil red. Never trusted either of them. My spleen hasn't stopped throbbing."

Magnolia and Glenda arrived in a flurry of scarves with plenty of opinions.

"Well, if this doesn't warrant a protest march in blooms of glory, I don't know what does," Magnolia declared, sticking a flower behind her ear.

"I say we start a preservation society," Glenda added. "With bylaws. And buttons."

Everyone locked up their stores and headed to the town hall meeting.

Inside *Town Hall*, the situation had escalated from simmering to boiling. Every seat in the council chamber was packed. More townsfolk crowded in the back and spilled into the hallway. A hand-painted banner had been hastily strung across the dais:

TOWN MEETING – ACTING MAYOR DOUG DELANEY
SPEAKS AT 4PM

Doug Delaney, now acting mayor by technicality, looked like he'd rather be anywhere else. His tie was crooked. He held a coffee mug that read WORLD'S #2 BOSS, and he cleared his throat so many times it sounded like he was tuning a kazoo.

"Fellow citizens of Wishville," he began, "I come to you today not just as assistant mayor but as a long-time member of this community and runner-up at the Town Chili Bowl."

A collective groan rippled across the chamber.

"Get to the well!" Gus yelled with a comb still wedged behind his ear.

"What's going to happen to the festival?" Bart called out, still wearing his apron. "And who's paying for all these paper lanterns if the mayor's been skimming the treasury?"

"Are we *still* getting fireworks?" Glenda asked.

Doug mopped sweat from his brow. "Yes. I mean—we're sorting through the budget right now, and rest assured, there will be...some kind of light display."

"You mean the mayor *gambled away* our festival fund?" Miss Ethel gasped. "That's sacred maple money!"

"Why wasn't anyone watching her?" Willa demanded. "Where was the oversight? The checks and balances?"

"I think the checks were bouncing," Tilly said grimly.

Doug tried to steady himself. "The council will meet tonight to determine the future of the festival and the preservation of the well. Until then, I assure you—there will be *no* bulldozers, no roller coasters, and *no* Mystic Taffy Tower."

Someone in the crowd blew their nose.

Another person wept quietly into their cider.

Outside, as the crowd spilled into the square in a frenzy of speculation, Evelyn Poe made her move. She glided toward Trip, who was currently leaning against a parking meter with one thumb hooked into a belt holster that held absolutely nothing of use—a sparkly badge, a wand flashlight, and a laminated "Citizen's Arrest Form."

Trip had grown a mustache over the winter and was now wearing mirrored sunglasses despite the cloud cover. He liked to patrol the gazebo after dark and had once ticketed his own cousin for "unlicensed moonwalking."

Evelyn approached like she was walking onto a movie set. "Trip," she said, with a feline smile. "You've been so...brave today. Keeping the peace and stepping up when it counts."

Trip tugged down his sunglasses just enough to make what he must assume was smoldering eye contact. "Justice doesn't take holidays, Miss Poe. Not on my watch."

"You know," she said, tilting her head, "I've always admired a man with a strong sense of order and...mystery."

Trip straightened to his full height, which wasn't very tall. "If you ever need a personal escort during these trying times, I *am* armed with intuition and three years of online crime scene forums."

Evelyn's smile widened. "I *do* enjoy a man with...experience. Samuel was such a boy compared to you."

From beside me, Vex let out a low growl. "She's aiming for a promotion. Self-appointed sheriff's wife is the next logical move."

"Poor Trip." I sighed. "He doesn't stand a chance."

"Neither does she," Vex replied. "He once arrested a trash can for loitering."

Holden joined us and we slipped away through the alley behind the *Town Hall*, toward the back of the community center where Rowan Baxter usually skulked. We found him pacing, his coat wrinkled, his expression tense. He jumped when we approached.

"You've got about five seconds to explain yourself," Holden said.

Rowan blinked. "You think I—?"

"We found moss on your gloves," I said, "the same kind as the well. And we know you were in Marin's office."

He swallowed, then reached into his bag and pulled out a small cloth-wrapped item: the voice recorder.

Holden's jaw tensed. "After gathering the evidence from it, I returned it to her. You stole it again?"

"I wanted to see if anything more was on it. I stole it the first time and set it up by the well," Rowan admitted. "Samuel was getting paranoid. He said he had proof the well was more than just folklore, but then he went quiet. I figured if I bugged the area, I might catch him...or at least figure out what he *wasn't* saying."

"You didn't listen to it?" I asked.

He shook his head. "No, I didn't dare go after it. After he died, I panicked. I didn't want to be linked to it, but I didn't hurt him. I swear."

Holden took the recorder, his tone flat. "Do me a favor and leave the investigating to the professionals."

Rowan's shoulders slumped. "I just wanted the truth."

"You and me both," I said. "Next time, try honesty first."

Vex padded to Rowan's feet and glared up at him. "Next time you touch something sacred, I'll mark your shoes. Permanently."

Rowan gaped. "Your cat talks?"

"He does a lot more than that," I said, "and he doesn't like being lied to."

Holden arched a brow at me and Vex, then he said to Rowan, "I didn't hear a thing. Go around saying cats talk will get you put away for being crazy."

"Got it. No talking cats. I'll keep my mouth shut." Rowan backed away warily.

"Good." Holden narrowed his eyes. "And I suggest in the future you keep your hands to yourself."

Nineteen

THE LATE AFTERNOON sun slanted through the birch trees like spilled gold, dappling the clearing around the well. Festival-goers meandered along the edge of the sacred grounds, drawn by curiosity more than reverence, sipping maple lemonade and lattes, and snapping photos of the mossy stones that ringed the well.

Children darted between booths with painted faces and sticky fingers, and the air was laced with woodsmoke, roasted nuts, and maple cotton candy. The faint, persistent fiddle music drifted in from the distant stage as people danced in front.

I stood near the path from the woods, my heart stuttering just a little as I watched the trees for movement. Not from worry— well, maybe a little from worry—but mostly from anticipation. I'd messaged Calderis with an update. At first, he wasn't happy about me sneaking Holden out of Elarion without a memory seal, but he'd finally agreed there was a greater benefit to keeping him as an ally. If Calderis could pull this off, we might finally get ahead of everything spiraling around us.

Beside me, Vex lounged on a sun-warmed boulder, his tail draped like a banner across the stone. He squinted toward the trees, his nose twitching slightly. "He's here," he said, his voice low and gravel-edged. "And I reminded him three times that ceremonial robes are not casual human attire. Let's hope it stuck."

Leaves rustled, branches shifted, and then he stepped out from the woods like some hero from a romance novel summoned by whispered need. I swallowed hard, never having seen him like this.

Calderis had traded his usual ethereal robes for snake-skin boots, dark jeans, a black Henley t-shirt, and a leather jacket. His thick silver hair was now a pale blond, no longer moving as if under water, and tied back in a man bun. His six-foot-ten-inch frame made the trees behind him look like props, and his bone structure could probably cut glass. His eyes, a sky blue in the fading light, scanned the festival with a mix of calculation and caution.

Holden met him halfway, playing it cool, but I saw the twitch at the corner of his mouth that said this was painful. "This is Detective Cal Deris," Holden said to the handful of townsfolk who had started to gather, using the tone of a man introducing a Hollywood heartthrob with a badge. "Boston Homicide," he added, clearing his hoarse throat. "Brought him in as a consultant on the Samuel Greer case."

"Pleasure to be here," Cal said, his voice a deep velvet rumble that practically parted the grass.

Dot gasped and fanned her face.

Belle clutched her cloak like she was about to faint.

Tilly dropped her journal.

"That man is a tall drink of *yes*," Belle whispered.

"He makes Holden look fun-sized," Dot added.

"He's what my spleen warned me about last week," Tilly said reverently. "A tower of deliciously divine trouble."

I bit my cheek to keep from laughing, though I couldn't disagree with them. He looked spectacular.

Holden looked like he wanted to melt into the soil.

Cal offered his hand, which Dot took like she'd found the Holy

Grail in a leather jacket. "Ladies," he said with an amused bow. "I've heard about your journey to Oz."

"Oh yes," Belle said, stepping forward and nudging Dot out of the way. "It was life-altering. I had a vision during that flight. The clouds formed a perfect map of ancient leylines around Wishville."

"And I saw my second husband," Dot added, bumping Belle to the side. "Turns out he's not dead...just inconveniently lost in Canada for twenty years now."

Cal smiled, looking entirely too at ease for a creature from a completely different world masquerading as a human cop. This was a side of him I hadn't seen in centuries. "Sounds like quite the adventure," he said, his full lips twitching slightly.

"It was," Tilly replied, flipping her notebook open as she stepped in front of the other two. "If the balloon weren't grounded, I'd insist you take a ride. You should see the well from above. It looks like a giant blue eye." She blinked way up at him and fluttered her lashes. "Nearly as blue as yours I do declare."

Cal tilted his head and smiled. "Perhaps once the repairs are complete, I'll take you up on that."

We turned toward the balloon, currently tethered and sagging slightly, its canvas belly deflated. Near the base, Eli and Sparks were elbow-deep in gears, tubing, and what looked like half of a grandfather clock.

"Lefty-loosey!" Sparks yelled, covered in soot and gripping a wrench like a dueling saber.

"I *am* going left!" Eli snapped back, wrestling with a valve.

"That's *my* left, not yours!"

"There is only one left, you walking spark plug!"

Weylan stood nearby, draped in his usual silk vest and reading poetry to the balloon. "She's temperamental today," he said without looking at anyone. "I suspect she heard rumors of the commercial redevelopment and lost the will to fly."

Vex sighed, speaking through my mind. *If this place gets any weirder, I might actually be the normal one.*

Cal leaned close to me as the Wellies began arguing about leylines versus cloud messages, a muscle in his jaw bulging. "What is Sparks doing here?"

"He's actually been a big help to me," I whispered back. "Same that Weylan has been for you."

He nodded once. "I'll allow it for now." His gaze swept the field, the edges of the well, and the festivalgoers with great interest. "We should speak somewhere quiet about the Council...and Thayn."

My smile faded. "Soon. But first let the town think you and Holden are just two detectives trying to solve a case. We need everyone to buy your story."

He glanced at Holden, who was fending off questions from Betsy, who was wielding a tray of fudge. "I supposed you're right," Cal said quietly. "Deception seems to be the currency of this town."

"Not always," I said. "Sometimes we use cookies."

Vex snorted.

We stood at the edge of the clearing, surrounded by laughter and flickering lights as the evening of day six settled over us. Underneath it all, I could feel the weight of the well behind us. The heartbeat of something old and sacred. The reason we were all pretending so hard to be normal.

And for the moment, Cal—six-foot-ten Elarion Dweller noble disguised as a human Boston homicide detective—fit right in.

That evening, the forest dimmed to a velvety dusk, the hush of twilight settling across Wishville like a comforting shawl. The last of the lanterns bobbed in the clearing as Calderis and I slipped away from the festival and made our way to my house near the edge of the woods in silence.

The walk was quiet but charged—not tense, exactly, but heavy with things unspoken. It wasn't lost on me that this was the first time in centuries I'd brought a man home. And certainly, the first time he *wasn't* human.

Inside, my house was warm, the hearth flickering with lazy amber flames. The scent of herbs, beeswax, and aged wood curled around us like a memory. Calderis took it all in—the hanging bundles of dried herbs, the mismatched mugs, the softly humming wind chimes made of glass and shell.

"Cozy," he murmured. "Different from our Elarion chambers."

I smiled faintly. "Different yet both a part of me."

Vex jumped onto the window seat, curling into a crescent of fur and shadow, but his eyes never left us.

Calderis set his borrowed badge on the side table and folded his tall frame into the armchair by the fire. He looked oddly comfortable there, a dream of a man carved from moonlight and forest lore, now inspecting a handmade Afghan like it was a price-less artifact. His gaze met mine and held me captive for far too long.

"We need a plan," I said, clearing my throat and perching on the edge of the sofa. "Something's happening at the crater. Weylan said the balloon picked up a heat signature from that direction again. That's what caused it to deflate."

Calderis's gaze sharpened. "A flare that size doesn't occur naturally in that part of the terrain. Unless someone used a stolen prototype..."

"I can take you there tomorrow," I offered.

He was already rising. "We need to go now." His eyes swirled like storm waters. "I sense a shift in energy. Something is happening."

I grabbed my jacket and led the way.

The woods had cooled significantly by the time we reached Hollow Glen. Moonlight trickled down through the canopy, striping the trail with silver. We heard the crackling before we saw it—the unmistakable sizzle of magic poorly handled.

A charred scent hung in the air.

We emerged onto the ridge overlooking the crater and froze.

Gavin Rhoades knelt in the dirt, his shirt singed and face streaked with ash and fear. He held a smoking monstrosity of a machine in his hands…it had to be the prototype. His knapsack lay discarded nearby, pages of notes fluttering like wounded birds. He stared off into the distance at moving shadows and noises.

My gaze followed his, and I sucked in a sharp breath.

Holden stood with fists clenched…fighting Eli!

Calderis clenched his fists, a low growl emerging from deep in his throat as he shouted, "Thayn!"

My jaw unhinged!

Calderis charged down the ridge and I followed as quickly as I could.

The man who'd been posing as Eli seemed to summon Pressure Command to crack the ground and destabilize the terrain. Holden leaped over the fissure, avoiding falling into the split. Summoning an Ember Pulse, he channeled molten energy, throwing Holden backward with a pulse of raw magic. Holden rolled, came up in a crouch, but his eyes widened as Thayn snarled and yanked off the black wig and beard, letting out an evil laugh. His gold Dweller hair gleamed like gemstones in the moonlight.

My heart sank.

How had I been so blind? He must have used a cloaking spell to hide his energy.

"You!" Holden shouted. "You're the one who—"

Calderis stepped forward, fury cloaked in ice. "You desecrated Elarion's trust, Thayn. You betrayed your people."

Gavin gasped. "I knew it! Elarion's real…and y-you're Dwellers. I knew this machine was dangerous. That's why I took it. H-He stole it from me and used it. I tried to stop him. I really did, but h-he was too strong for me."

Thayn smiled, the cruel twist of someone who knew the game had already moved on. "You weak humans. You're no match for me." His hard gaze landed on Calderis. "And you. You're no detective. You think you've won, *Cal Deris*? You're too late. The rebellion has already begun. You can't seal a crack once it bursts open."

With a roar, Calderis used Obsidian Crafting to conjure a scepter and shield from the earth's cooled magma and lunged. Their clash was elemental—fire and ice, power and precision. Thayn moved with desperation, using Ember Pulses, but Calderis was superior with righteousness honed by centuries of control. Magic shimmered between them in stinging bursts.

Magma Ward allowed me to summon protective heat barriers to shield Gavin and Holden from the flying debris.

Then Calderis struck true.

A crystalline pulse exploded from his scepter, knocking Thayn flat. The traitor groaned, his body crackling with restrained energy. Calderis conjured enchanted bindings from thin air and secured Thayn's wrists behind him. "By the authority of Elarion, you are my prisoner and will be punished accordingly."

Thayn hissed, but the fight had gone from his eyes.

"Gavin." I looked him in the eyes. "I appreciate your help in trying to keep Wishville safe."

He sat slumped against a boulder, still dazed and trembling. His eyes darted around the scorched earth, his breath short and uneven. His hands trembled as they still clutched the smoking prototype. "I saw...I saw real magic," he whispered hoarsely. "Calderis, Eli, and...you. You're all—"

"I know what you saw," I said gently, brushing soot from his sleeve as I carefully took the prototype from his hands, "but you won't remember it."

His brows knit. "Wait, what do you—?"

I touched his temple lightly, whispering the incantation under my breath.

Vex sat beside us, his tail curled, watching solemnly. "A kindness, really," he purred.

"Trust me, he's better off not knowing. Can't tell people what you can't remember." Amber light pooled beneath my fingertips, swirling once, then vanishing into Gavin's skin like an infusion.

Holden took the prototype and put it in an evidence bag.

Gavin's lashes fluttered. He blinked up at me, confused. "What happened? I feel like I fell...?"

"You did," I said with a soft smile. "You had a bit of an accident. You tripped while hiking near the crater. Gave us all quite a scare."

He rubbed the back of his head. "Right...yeah. That's probably it."

Calderis nodded approvingly from the shadows. "We'll get him back to town." And with that, the memory of what Gavin saw faded into nothingness, just another mystery lost to the fog of Wishville.

We returned to town under the cover of night. The festival grounds were winding down, but the clearing still buzzed with streetlights and lingering families savoring their hot mulled cider and stories.

Holden walked beside Calderis, who now carried himself not as a stranger, but as a soldier with a duty fulfilled. Sparks noticed us first. His eyes darted to the bound man and widened.

Weylan, standing near the balloon with his usual theatrical air, tipped his head in solemn understanding.

"Foreign fugitive," Calderis announced to the curious few. "Wanted on multiple counts abroad. Being extradited tonight."

A murmur rose.

Sparks saluted him with a wrench. "Nicely done, Detective Deris."

Weylan laid a hand on his heart and said, "May the wind carry justice swiftly."

I looked at Calderis, saw the weariness hidden in the corners of his eyes, and knew that this wasn't over. The rebellion had started. The treaty was fractured. The surface and the realm below had never been closer to shattering. But for tonight, at least, we had won a battle.

And I wasn't alone in the fight.

CHAPTER
Twenty

AS THE FESTIVAL lights dimmed and the music faded into twilight, Calderis left with Thayn in custody, a shroud of quiet satisfaction in his wake. The crowd dispersed slowly, reluctant to let go of the final sparkle of celebration, unaware of the monumental confrontation that had just taken place beneath their noses.

Holden and I watched him disappear into the woods, with Vex perched on my shoulder. Just as we turned to leave, a voice called out from behind us.

"Detective Thorn! Ms. Wells! Wait up." Dr. Ethan Bellamy, Wishville's medical examiner, jogged toward us with a manila envelope tucked under one arm and concern etched across his face. His red hair was tousled from the wind, and his wire-rimmed glasses sat slightly askew. "I was looking all over for you," he said, catching his breath. "Didn't think I'd find you still here."

Holden straightened. "What's going on?"

"It's Samuel," Bellamy said, holding out the envelope. "The autopsy report finally came in and...well, it's strange. Very strange." He opened the file and handed it to Holden, who began flipping through the pages, his brow furrowing with every line.

I peeked over his shoulder.

"Frozen?" Holden echoed. "Not from the cold snap?"

Bellamy shook his head. "His tissue damage and cellular crystallization patterns are consistent with flash freezing. Something artificial. Not weather-related."

My heart dropped. "Then someone used something like dry ice," I said out loud, and thought, *Or magic.*

Holden's eyes darkened. "You said it happened at the well. Who else was there that morning?"

I thought back. "Stan McDuff. He was collecting cans for the recycling tent, sleep sorting them. He does that sometimes, especially when under the influence. He mumbled something about hearing something unusual...and the well having an eye and looking back at him."

Bellamy gave a noncommittal shrug. "It's not a smoking gun, but Stan does have access to industrial-grade dry ice. He picks it up from the food supply drop-offs when he does bottle returns. Sells it to locals for their parties. It keeps their drinks cold for much longer than regular ice."

"Thanks, Doc." Holden turned to me. "Let's find him."

It didn't take long.

We spotted Stan near the edge of the square, methodically sorting aluminum cans into colored bins. His overalls were smeared with something that could be either paint or festival caramel, and he wore his signature ratty fisherman's hat.

"Stan," Holden called. Stan looked up, blinking slowly like a man who had just awakened from a particularly philosophical nap.

"Detective. Lyra. Cat." He nodded at Vex. "What does the can say today?"

Vex purred for my ears only. *It says answer our questions before I claw your socks off.*

"Stan," I said gently, stepping forward. "I saw you at the well the morning Samuel died. Do you remember?"

Stan squinted at a crushed can in his hand. "The can says...yes."

Holden crossed his arms. "Tell me again what you saw that morning?"

"I saw someone moving like fog and speaking like thunder. I thought it was the well come to life."

"You thought Samuel was the well?" I asked.

"I think so." Stan squinted. "He had eyes. Too many eyes. You know what they say—'When the wishing well stares back, your secrets bubble to the surface.'"

Vex muttered, "That is not a thing anyone says."

"Did your cat just talk?" Stan stared at Vex.

"He has a strange meow," I said.

Holden knelt beside the bins. "Did you touch Samuel when you saw him? Did you do anything to him, Stan?"

Stan tapped the side of his head. "He was raving about the portal opening soon. Said he knew everything. I just wanted him to hush. Just...hush. So, I told him he should chill out."

"Did you use dry ice to help him chill out?" I asked, cold flooding my veins.

Stan looked down at the crushed can again. "The can says...maybe."

Holden sighed. "We're going to need to take a statement. Come with us."

"This late? Can't it wait until morning? I need to pack up the recyclables."

"I'll send someone for them."

Stan shrugged. "Do you think I'll still be able to go to the aluminum poetry night?"

"Let's take this one step at a time." Holden guided him away.

I stayed behind with Vex curling around my ankles like a coiled ribbon. "What do you think?" I asked him quietly.

"I think he's not intentionally malicious," Vex said, "but he may have caused more damage than he realizes."

Or something else did...

～

The clock by my bedside read 2:17 a.m. when the pulse of Dweller magic slid over my skin like a cool mist. I sat bolt upright, my breath catching in my throat.

Calderis.

A soft shimmer danced over the far wall—one only visible to me, the Guardian of the Well—and I recognized it instantly as his private summoning when he didn't want to risk using our Elarion phones.

He was calling me to Elarion.

I had sent him an orb update before falling asleep that Samuel had been unnaturally frozen. The autopsy confirmed it. The surface world was unraveling, and now Calderis had something to share in return.

I threw off the covers and dressed quickly, sliding into my dressiest ceremonial robes that shimmered like starlight and fog. The fabric whispered against my skin, cool and humming with ancient energy.

Vex leaped onto the windowsill and tilted his head. "It's Calderis, isn't it?" he asked, his voice still heavy with sleep.

I nodded. "He wants to meet. He knows something."

"Of course he does. Dwellers and their dramatic timing," he muttered. "Are we bringing Holden?"

"Yes. He deserves to hear this." I picked up my cell phone and called.

It rang three times.

"Lyra?" Holden's voice was a gravelly rasp of half-sleep and confusion. "Everything okay?"

"I need you to meet me at the well. Something's happened. Calderis summoned me so it must be urgent."

He paused a beat, and then said, "On my way."

By the time I reached the well under my Moonveil, the stars shone brightly and the clearing was hushed, blanketed in moonlight. The whisper of trees surrounded the sacred stones.

Holden arrived minutes later in jeans and a hoodie. "Wow, you look...just wow."

My lips tipped up slightly at the corners. "Thank you. You look...camouflaged."

He chuckled, holding a duffel in one hand. "This isn't my standard detective disguise," he said, "but nothing is standard about our lives right now."

He stepped to the well's edge, and I began the ritual chant.

The waters shimmered deep in the well and then parted like silk as the grate vanished, revealing the swirling portal beneath. I nodded to him as I stepped through, and he followed.

In Elarion, the luminous sky flickered with silver clouds, and the faint scent of violet moss and charged crystal greeted us. Holden stumbled a bit before steadying himself and stepped behind the tree that hid the ceremonial robes Calderis had given him. He changed and stashed his duffel in its place then emerged, looking ethereal.

"You clean up okay," I said with a smirk.

He grunted. "I feel like a cosplay wizard, but it's fine."

Calderis met us at the threshold of the veil gardens, his expression grave. A cloak draped over his shoulders like a shadow, and his eyes gleamed like frozen storm light. He nodded once to Holden and then turned his gaze onto me.

"You came," he said, his voice dipping softer than normal. "Thank you."

I stepped forward. "You said it was urgent."

"It is. Come. Selvi is waiting."

We followed him through a corridor of luminous columns and into the deeper chambers of the city. Selvi sat curled on a marble bench beneath a cascading wall of starlight vines. Her hands were clasped tightly, her silver-streaked ice blue hair draped over one shoulder like liquid frost, her expression etched with anguish. She looked up, and for once, her eyes held no mystery—only pale blue pain.

"What's wrong?" I asked.

Her eyes filled with tears. "I saw the vision weeks ago before Samuel's death. A mortal man would tear open the veil between our worlds. War would follow, and there would be death on both sides. I didn't know who the man was until word spread of Samuel's findings."

"Who told you about Samuel's findings?" I asked.

"It doesn't matter," she responded.

Holden's brows drew together. "What did you do, Selvi?"

"I tried to warn Samuel to stop, especially after he stole the wish token. When he wouldn't, I tried to frighten him," she whispered. "I conjured the cold around him, meaning only to freeze the moment—to make him stop and question everything. But...I'd never used it on a mortal before. I misjudged his strength."

"Oh, Selvi," I whispered.

She looked up at Calderis. "I never meant to kill him. I swear it. But he froze too fast, and I left before he thawed."

The chamber went still.

Even the vines seemed to hold their shimmer.

Holden let out a slow breath. "You panicked."

Selvi's voice broke. "And now I wake every day with his last breath echoing in my bones. He died because of me." Her voice hitched and a small sob slipped out. "I don't think Seris will ever forgive me."

Calderis's jaw tensed. He crossed to her with the measured grace of someone holding back a tide of emotion. "You've committed a crime, Selvi. Regardless of your intent."

She bowed her head. "I know. I've already imprisoned myself in guilt, but if justice must follow, I won't run."

He raised his hand, and from the shadows stepped Drelian.

"Take her into custody," Calderis said. His voice was steady. Too steady.

Drelian moved forward and took Selvi by the arm.

She didn't resist. Just turned to me as she passed and whispered, "The flame of regret burns colder than ice."

Then she was gone, swallowed into the corridors of Elarion's justice.

I looked to Calderis. There was no triumph in his face. No peace. Just sorrow.

"You knew her well," I said quietly.

"Since we were children," he replied. "She was an orphan. Her mother was killed by a human back during the war when her weakness was discovered, and her father was never known. She was once the brightest seer of our realm, and now...this."

Holden touched my elbow, standing beside me. "So that's it? The case is solved."

"Yes," I said, "and just in time. It's officially day seven of WishFest. The wish is now cleared from the well so the well can choose a recipient by the end of the night, and the treaty should be restored." I turned toward the glowing pools that lined the floor. Their reflections flickered with moments from lives that were never whole.

Calderis stood on the other side of me with his hand on my shoulder. "Your world—ours...neither is as perfect as we want to believe."

"No," I agreed softly, "but truth lives in the cracks, and we finally have it."

We stood there in silence, three souls linked by sorrow, justice, and the fragile hope that something brighter might grow from the darkness. Holden's hand tightened slightly on my arm, and Calderis's gaze returned to the hall where Selvi had been taken. The balance had shifted. The treaty might hold—for now.

But beneath the veil, both worlds were still trembling.

CHAPTER
Twenty~One

THE FINAL MORNING of WishFest dawned bright and suspiciously perfect—as if the town itself was trying to convince us that everything was fine. Blue skies, sunshine, and just enough breeze to make the bunting snap cheerfully from the lampposts. The smell of cinnamon buns, roasted pecans, and lemon-zested waffles hung in the air like bait, but I could still feel the undercurrent of tension.

The hush beneath the cheer.

The questions we hadn't really answered.

Vex was draped across my shoulders like a living scarf, his tail flicking every few seconds with barely concealed agitation. I couldn't blame him. Today felt like a performance. The town needed closure, and Holden and I had given them a story.

Now we just had to sell it.

A crowd had already gathered on the central green, where the closing ceremony was set to take place. Townsfolk milled about in festival garb—sunhats, ribbon sashes, and face paint left over from the fairy parade. The booths were open again, although the vendors worked with the stiff smiles of people trying not to talk about the murder that had clouded the entire festival. You could feel the tension in the air.

"Morning, Ms. Wells." Betsy Plum handed me a paper cup of espresso with extra foam, just the way I liked it. "You holding up?"

"Barely," I said with a tired smile. "Last day."

She patted my shoulder. "You done good, honey."

I nodded my thanks and looked toward the makeshift stage. The interim mayor fussed with his cue cards, flanked by the town council members and a local teen tasked with holding a clipboard and trying not to sweat through her dress.

Holden was already in position, standing at the edge of the stage, his arms folded and posture rigid. His eyes found mine immediately. We hadn't spoken much since we agreed on the story, but we didn't need to.

Selvi was real, they just didn't need to know she was a Dweller.

We'd stuck as close to the truth as possible. The real Selvi had crossed the veil to scare Samuel with her frost magic but had tragically frozen him to death at the well. Maybe it had been an accident. Maybe not. All we knew for certain was we couldn't tell the town that one of the mythical beings from under the well had done it.

So, we gave them Selvi the obsessed outsider.

According to our official story, she was a mentally unstable tourist who'd been trying to disrupt the festival, convinced that stopping the celebrations would "awaken the well's true power." She'd used dry ice then panicked and fled. Detective Cal Deris had secured her extradition, and Stan was cleared of any wrongdoing.

We told them she was gone along with Eli.

The eccentric people of Wishville, in their love for spectacle and their hunger for magic, mostly believed us. Of course, they had to speculate.

"Oh, I bet it was that woman with the sequin turban from day two," whispered Fiona. "Remember? She had that mysterious cough and kept talking to the well like it was answering her."

"No, no, it had to be the gal in the green poncho," said Gus. "She was loitering near the petting zoo and asking if the well could heal 'soul decay.' Freaked me right out."

"I think it was that blogger from Boston with the giant hat and the emotional support lizard," said Magnolia.

Behind them, the Wellies had arrived in full flair, fanning the flames of speculation with wild abandon. Dot wore a cape covered in polka dots and wish ribbons and was carrying a sign that read *'Guard the Well, Ban the Unseen'*. Belle had attached tiny mirrors to her sleeves to "deflect ill intent." And Tilly had brought her journal, claiming it had twitched when "Selvi's energy passed through town."

"I still say she wasn't human," Dot announced to no one and everyone. "No dry ice could do that kind of damage without ruining your hair."

"Her aura must've been split," Belle said solemnly. "Probably saw too many lifetimes and forgot which one she was in."

"I had a dream about it," Tilly added. "She was wearing socks with sandals. That's how I *knew*."

I fought a sigh and sipped my coffee. All we could do now was wait.

Holden approached me, his steps crisp on the cobblestone. "You okay?"

"Define okay."

He gave a one-shouldered shrug. "You think they're buying it?"

"They're already rewriting it in their heads." I glanced toward Dot, who was now drawing a diagram on the sidewalk with pink chalk. "That's Wishville for you."

Holden grunted, then handed me a folded paper. "The mayor's statement. He wants us to read this."

I unfolded it and scanned the carefully curated script. Samuel's name was mentioned once, "the tragic incident involving a concerned researcher." Then came the official line, "Thanks to swift investigative work and the assistance of outside authorities, the individual responsible—an outsider named Selvi—has been apprehended and is no longer a threat. We now move forward, honoring our traditions, grateful for another successful WishFest."

I folded the paper again and held it like it might burn me. "He really thinks this will end the gossip?" I asked.

"No," Holden said, "but he thinks it will give people enough closure to move on."

"And the well?" I asked softly. "Do you think it will choose a wish to grant?"

Holden looked toward the clearing where the stone ring glistened in the morning light. "If you had asked me that a week ago, I would have thought you were crazy. Now, I hope the well chooses a recipient for the sake of both our worlds."

We took our places as the mayor stepped up to the mic.

"Good citizens of Wishville," he called out, his voice reverberating across the festival grounds. "Today, we conclude another magical WishFest—one filled with beauty, creativity, and, yes, challenge."

A pause increased the tension.

"As you all know, we suffered a tragedy this past week. But thanks to the swift work of our law enforcement and visiting authorities, justice has been served."

He glanced at us and gave a nod.

Holden stepped forward. He didn't read the paper. He spoke plainly in his own words and with authority. "Samuel Greer's murder has been solved, may he rest in peace. This well is special to our town and the festival is so important to many. May one of you be lucky enough to have your wish come true this season. Good luck to you all." He stepped back.

The well responded.

A gurgle sounded and then water rushed back in, filling the well. The crowd hushed. Even the Wellies went still. Vex straightened on my shoulder. The water stopped rising, and then everything went silent once more.

Gasps and murmurs rang out, some speculating the magic was real while others believed it was purely coincidental.

"A sign," Tilly whispered.

"The well's ready," Dot said with conviction.

"New wish recipient incoming," Belle added, already scribbling predictions in her glitter-covered notebook.

Holden met my eyes, and relief flickered in his.

"I hope that means it worked," I whispered.

"Either that or the damage I suspect Henry's crew did to the grounds has been restored," he murmured.

I nodded, choosing to have hope. Because, beneath the cheers and applause, the real story remained buried. Samuel's wish had hopefully been cleared after his murder was solved, opening the well to choosing a new wish. The treaty was fragile. The portal beneath the well was still vulnerable.

And time was running out.

Evening fell like a shroud, the last rays of sunlight bleeding into purples and blues as the final day of WishFest drifted toward its reluctant close. Paper lanterns bobbed gently along the clearing, casting halos of light across the cobblestones. Music played from a nearby bandstand—a wistful fiddle tune accompanied by the soft rhythm of clapping hands—but it all felt muted. Hollow. Because the well still hadn't chosen.

No shimmer.

No pulse of light.

No new wish drawn.

I paced the clearing, scanning the crowd for any clue. My dress, a flowing shade of moonlight silver and long hair hanging free as a nod to the world I came from, felt like too much against the knot building in my chest. Vex was nowhere in sight, which unnerved me more than I wanted to admit.

He never disappeared this long without reason, or when he was with Fenrin.

I ducked behind the food stalls and past the last row of artisan tents, making my way toward the woods that bordered the festival grounds. The scent of damp earth and woodsmoke rose around me as I stepped beneath the first canopy of leaves. The music grew faint. The laughter dimmed. And I could feel it.

Something was wrong.

A prickle rose on the back of my neck, and I turned slowly.

"I expected you'd come looking," said a voice, smooth and cold.

I gasped. It couldn't be.

Drelian emerged from the trees like a shadow given flesh, his gleaming frostbitten stars for eyes dulled to a pale blue. His aquamarine hair, now different shades of blond, was damp from the humidity, and his hands clenched into fists at his sides.

"You shouldn't be here." I tried to keep my voice steady. "This is sacred ground. You might upset the balance and the well won't choose."

"Sacred?" he echoed with a scoff. "You think this town—this *festival*—is sacred? It's a masquerade built on stolen wishes and broken promises. There is no balance. The treaty favors humans. It never should have been formed."

My breath caught as realization hit me hard. "The well hasn't chosen because the real killer hasn't been caught. *You're* behind everything. You ordered Selvi to kill Samuel, didn't you?"

Drelian stepped closer, the air around him crackling with latent power. "She was supposed to kill him with intent," he said. "She tried to scare him. Silence him before he uncovered the truth. He died, but accidentally. She was weak like her mother."

I blinked. "Her mother?"

He bared his teeth in something that might have once been a smile but was now pure evil. "My father had two families. One with my mother, his *wife*. And one with Selvi's mother, his *mistress.* Selvi was my half-sister. My secret. Even Calderis never knew."

Shock coursed through me like an electric jolt.

"She did everything to earn my favor," Drelian went on, his voice tightening. "Trained in secret. Learned to channel ice magic like our father. I hated her, but I knew I could use her. I told her what she wanted to hear. That she could be more than just a footnote in our world. That together we could change it. But she was too soft. She begged me to let her try her way, and she failed."

He looked at me with such raw bitterness it made my skin crawl. "She couldn't finish the job, and it killed her inside. You took her from me."

I shook my head. "No, Drelian. You took her from yourself. You twisted her love into a weapon."

He snarled and lunged—but a blur of movement cut between us.

Holden.

"Back off," he barked, positioning himself in front of me.

Drelian's lips curled. "Ah, the mortal pet." His eyes filled with a magma internal glow.

Holden didn't flinch. "If you so much as breathe wrong, I'll—"

Drelian lifted a hand and summoned a Storm Veil of a choking mist. The wind shifted violently. Branches snapped. Leaves spiraled. Holden covered his mouth and eyes, coughing uncontrollably. That was when Drelian attacked, blasting him with a force that caused Holden to fly backward and slam into a tree with a groan of pain, clutching his arm.

"You really think you're a match for me?" Drelian laughed evilly.

"Stop!" I cried, running to Holden's side.

Drelian stalked forward, his hands glowing faintly with crackling energy. "I should have dealt with you both long ago. You and Calderis ruined everything. I should be Chief Enforcer like my father by now. And Calderis—he was *meant* to follow his father as Chief Elder, but he turned his back on the old ways. On *me.*"

"You don't get to decide destiny." I stepped between him and Holden.

Drelian's laugh was bitter. "Don't I? I've spent decades building this rebellion. Thayn was just a pawn. A devout fool who worshipped the old vision. *I* gave the orders. I built the cracks in the treaty one whisper at a time." He turned at the sound of new footsteps.

Calderis.

The Dweller Chief stood at the edge of the glade, his eyes wide with shock. "Drelian..." he whispered. "Why?"

Drelian's face twisted. "Because I was born for it. We trained together, studied together, and bled together, but you were always chosen. I had to *earn* every scrap of respect, while you sat on a throne you didn't even want."

"I never knew," Calderis said, his voice raw.

"No," Drelian hissed. "You were too busy being righteous. You thought the treaty made us strong, but all it did was make us compliant. Cowards."

Calderis stepped forward slowly. "Selvi was your sacrifice, wasn't she?"

"She was my legacy!" Drelian roared. "She was mine to command, but you took that from me, too. And all because you couldn't see the world I was trying to build."

He launched forward with a cry of rage, striking Calderis with a blast of raw energy. Calderis stumbled back, shielding himself, but Drelian was fast, relentless. Their magic clashed like colliding storms—ice and air and heat searing through the glade. Trees bent. Roots cracked. The very earth trembled.

Calderis was losing.

I saw it in the slump of his shoulders, the stagger of his steps.

"No," I whispered. "Not like this." I stepped forward, summoning every ounce of power that pulsed inside me. The well. My mother. My Dweller blood.

Raising my hands, I used Skycall to make the birds swarm between the men, separating them, and with a flick of the wrist I sent a wind gust to carry Calderis to safety. Waiting for a clean shot, I tapped into every ounce of my magic to strike a blow. Light burst from my palms—a radiant wave of hot amber gold energy that nailed Drelian in the chest and knocked him off his feet. He hit the ground hard, stunned. His eyes widened in disbelief as he clutched his steaming chest.

I stepped over him, my hands still glowing. "You underestimated me," I said softly.

He snarled. "You think this is over? The rebellion lives on. No wish was chosen. The treaty will never survive? You failed, Lyra Wells."

I looked at the sky. "There's still time."

"You will face judgement before the Council, my friend." Calderis limped forward, blood trailing down his leg. "It's over."

"I'll tell them you let a human into Elarion," he spat.

"I'm prepared to face my father's wrath." Calderis stood straighter, holding his head high with honor. "The outcome was worth the risk."

Drelian looked at him—really looked—and for the first time I saw pain in his eyes. Not rage. Not pride. Grief. "I thought we were building the future together," he rasped.

"You were building something," Calderis said, "but it wasn't a future...and it wasn't with me."

Drelian dropped his head. "Then do what you must."

I bound him with a spell of containment, wrapping energy around him like chains.

He didn't resist.

Calderis approached slowly, placing a hand on his former friend's shoulder. "The Council will decide your fate."

Drelian looked up, his gaze empty. "Then I suppose I'll finally be remembered for something." He vanished with Calderis in a shimmer of light, leaving only scorched leaves and broken branches behind.

I dropped to my knees beside Holden, who groaned as he sat up.

"Are you okay?" I asked, brushing dirt from his face.

"It's my shoulder, but I'll live. Next time," he said, wincing, "remind me not to pick fights with rebel Dwellers...and definitely not with half-blood Guardians."

I let out a shaky laugh and leaned into him, letting the adrenaline bleed out of my bones.

Above us, the sky cleared—and in the distance, a light pulsed.

The well.

A shimmer of silver rose above the festival.

It had chosen at last.

CHAPTER
Twenty~Two

THE MORNING after WishFest felt like waking from a dream. Mist hung low over the grass, curling in silvery ribbons across the grounds, and the rising sun painted everything in a golden wash, soft and forgiving. The crisp scent of dew mixed with the sweet remnants of maple, melting fudge, and lavender-sugar dust that clung stubbornly to every surface.

The music had stopped, the floats were gone, but traces of joy still lingered in the air like perfume from a departed guest. Cleanup had begun before dawn. Staffers and volunteers in wrinkled festival shirts moved across the grounds with tired but content expressions, stacking folding chairs, rolling up banners, and dismantling booths with practiced ease.

Streamers trailed from trees like exhausted dancers. Confetti glittered in sidewalk cracks. One poor helium balloon vendor was wrangling the last of his balloons, which had tangled themselves around a lamppost like mischievous spirits unwilling to go home.

I stood quietly near the well. It was draped in garlands half-wilted from the night's chill, no more shimmer or glow and water levels back to normal. My fingers brushed over its edge, and for a moment, I closed my eyes and listened.

Nothing stirred from below.

Not the Dweller realm. Not my mother's voice. Not even Vex, who, for once, had vanished before dawn without explanation. Probably to see Fenrin. He cared for her more than he cared to admit. Still, I felt something in the air. Not tension exactly, but anticipation. Like the town was holding its breath, waiting to hear who the lucky wish recipient would be.

"Think we'll ever get through one of these without any drama?" I murmured to no one in particular.

Vex returned just then—silent as a ghost—padding along the well's edge before leaping gracefully onto my shoulder, his tail looping lazily around my neck. I should have known he would appear when I needed him. He always did.

He purred low in his throat, then muttered, "Where's the fun in that?"

I smiled, but it faded as I looked back toward the festival grounds. The well had chosen someone last night. I'd seen the shimmer rise—silver light twisting upward like ribbon caught in wind, but no one had come forward yet. They weren't required to, of course, but usually the recipient was so excited they couldn't help themselves.

So far...silence.

It was as if the magic had paused mid-sentence, and for a moment, I grew worried.

Until someone came sprinting across the grounds in orthopedic sneakers and unmatched socks, waving a handbag like a flag. "Lyra! Lyra, it happened!"

It took a moment to register what I was seeing. Miss Ethel, practically flying across the trampled grass, her cheeks pink, a daisy tucked behind one ear, and her green cardigan flapping like a cape.

"It worked!" she shouted, nearly bowling me over. "Oh, honey, it *worked!*"

I caught her by the elbows. "Ethel, breathe. What worked?"

"My wish! My *WISH!*" she squealed, her eyes shining behind her bifocals. "I didn't tell anyone—I didn't want to jinx it—but I dropped my note into the well on the third day. You remember? I was standing right there, clutching my thermos of peppermint brandy—er, *tea*—and I said, 'Please bring my Tasha home. Let her come back and open her pie shop like she always dreamed.' And now—*she's here!* Monsier Buttons and Madame Frizzle are going to be so excited!"

A car door slammed in the distance, and there she was.

Tasha Frimble, Ethel's granddaughter, stepped onto the festival grounds, dragging two enormous suitcases and carrying a neon pink pie carrier. She wore yoga pants, sneakers, and a t-shirt that read *Eat Pie, Not Feelings.* Her hair was pulled into a messy bun, her cheeks windburned, and her smile?

Pure sunshine.

"Grandma Ethel!" she called, lifting the pie carrier over her head like a trophy. "I'm home!"

The townsfolk cleaning up erupted into applause.

Willa gasped and clutched her coffee. "She hasn't set foot in Wishville in a *decade.*"

Gus jabbed the air with his comb. "She swore she'd *never* leave the city. Said this town was too small for her dreams."

"And yet she's back," said Belle, her eyes twinkling, "with pastry."

"I *knew* it!" Dot declared, swaying in with her sequin polka dot cape and divining teacup. "I *knew* the well had one more miracle in it."

"You did not," Tilly huffed. "You said she was moving to Italy to open a cannoli bar."

"Same concept." Dot sniffed.

Tasha ran into her grandmother's arms and the two spun, laughing and crying, and dropping at least one container of whipped cream onto the grass. Cheers went up around the clearing. Strangers clapped. Betsy Plum handed out coffee and biscotti. Even the skeptical old head of the town council cracked a smile.

Everyone wanted to believe in something again.

I turned my face toward the morning sun and let out a breath I hadn't realized I'd been holding. The treaty was intact. The town was healing. And for now, Elarion and Dwellers were back to being just legends and folklore.

A tap on my shoulder made me turn to find Interim Mayor Doug Delaney—clipboard in hand, sweater vest rumpled, comb-over crooked—smiling like he'd just aced a spelling bee. "Lyra, can you join me on the bandstand for a quick announcement?" he asked.

I nodded, following him toward the rickety platform where town proclamations were made and parades were launched. Doug stepped to the mic and tapped it until it squawked.

"People of Wishville," he said, gesturing around at the crowd, "thank you all for making this year's WishFest unforgettable. Despite...a few hiccups," he glanced at me meaningfully, "we've come through stronger than ever."

Murmurs of agreement rippled through the crowd.

Doug held up a sheet of paper. "I'd like to share some wonderful news. Thanks to the town-wide petition led by none other than Lyra Wells—and signed by most of you—we are offi-cially keeping WishFest as a *seasonal* event. That means we'll cele-brate four times a year: spring, summer, fall, and winter."

A beat of silence hummed, and then the clearing *exploded* with cheers.

Someone popped a leftover confetti cannon. The Wellies started an impromptu kazoo rendition of the Wishville anthem. Miss Ethel yelled, "Pie for everyone!" and Tasha started handing out slices like Oprah giving away cars.

Doug grinned, then stepped aside for the one man no one expected to see on that stage.

Chief Holden Thorn. He took the mic with one hand, the other arm in a sling from his injured shoulder, his posture straight and expression unreadable. But his voice, when it came, was firm.

"As you all know I'm not exactly known for being a fan of glitter or gnomes or papier-mâché unicorns," he said.

A ripple of laughter rose.

"I still think the festival invites crime, but I've also seen the good it brings out in people. What it *means* to this town. And even if I'll never be caught in a fairy-wing costume," more laughter rang out, "I can say with confidence, I am no longer in opposition."

Gasps sounded.

Applause thundered.

Glenda fainted again.

"I support the seasonal festivals," Holden finished. "WishFest isn't just a celebration. It's a reminder of who we are, and what we're willing to believe in."

My heart swelled so suddenly it hurt. He looked at me then—really looked—and I saw something in his eyes that hadn't been there before. Trust...and something else that made my cheeks burn.

As the crowd broke into a spontaneous chorus of, "Wishing On a Star," I stepped down from the stage.

Vex leaped off my shoulder and waltzed around like royalty.

"You did it," Betsy whispered, pressing a coffee refill into my hand.

"No," I said, my gaze sweeping over the crowd of happy people, "*we* did it."

The well had chosen. The wish had come true. And maybe—just maybe—everything would finally be okay.

The well pulsed once—softly, like the exhale of an ancient dream—and I felt the tug immediately. It was late that evening, and I was in my kitchen when it happened, halfway through a slice of leftover pie and nursing a mug of tea that had long since gone cold. The silver spiral pendant around my neck glowed faintly, and the wind outside shifted, curling around the edges of my home like a whisper.

A summons.

Vex lifted his head from the cushion by the hearth, his one blue and one green eyes narrowing. "They're calling."

I didn't need to ask who.

I text Holden and ten minutes later, we stood beside the well. The sky above was star-flecked velvet, the clearing quiet save for the rustling trees and the hush of crickets. His eyes met mine in silent understanding as we stepped forward together. No hesitation. No time for fear. I whispered the incantation.

The well shimmered, and we fell through.

We landed in Elarion and followed the moss path, turning in another direction that led to a path of polished obsidian, its surface glittering with veins of luminous blue. In this part of Elarion, the golden orbs overhead were dim like a flag at half-mast as if something important were happening. Bioluminescent vines crawled up marble columns, and waterfalls poured into slow, twinkling streams.

Holden straightened beside me, visibly tense as he rubbed his shoulder but trying not to show it. "Still not used to any of this," he muttered.

"I don't think you're supposed to be," I said gently.

Ahead of us, Calderis waited—impeccably dressed in black and deep green, his face solemn, but something flickered in his eyes when he saw me. Relief, maybe. Or something more complicated. "This way," he said, his voice lower than usual. "Vaerion is waiting."

He led us into the *Hall of Harmony*, a towering cathedral of carved crystal and woven silver threads where important treaties and pacts were made. The Council of Elders sat in their crescent ring of thrones, each one clad in colorful robes that shifted like oil on water.

At their center stood Vaerion—Chief Elder, arbiter of the treaty, and father to Calderis.

I was intimidated every time I met him, tonight was no exception. Tonight, he radiated the still, commanding energy of someone who had spent centuries bearing the weight of decisions that shaped both worlds. His silver-white hair gently moved beneath his deep sapphire hood, and when he turned those pale blue eyes to Holden, the temperature of the room seemed to drop.

"You brought a mortal across, Lyra Wells," Vaerion said, his voice like polished stone. "Know that this defies the laws we have kept for centuries."

"He's not just a mortal." I stepped forward with my back straight and chin held high. "He's my ally. He protected the treaty, fought for this town, and risked his life in ways that some Dwellers haven't."

Vaerion's gaze sharpened, a flinty edge behind the cold calm. "He has seen too much. He knows secrets that must remain hidden. It would be simpler, safer—for both realms—to erase what he knows."

Holden stiffened beside me but didn't speak.

"No," I said firmly. "You can't."

A few of the Elders murmured, but I didn't waver.

"If you take that from him," I said, "you're not just erasing knowledge. You're erasing trust. And the treaty—the very idea of it—depends on trust between both sides. Between us."

I felt Calderis step closer behind me, his voice soft but unwavering. "She's right," he said. "Holden Thorn may be human, but he's proven his worth a hundred times over. He's not a liability. He's an asset."

Vaerion's eyes flicked between the two of us, then landed on Calderis. "And you, my son," he said with a note of weary sadness, "once trusted your best friend like a brother, and look how he betrayed you. How do I know you won't be led astray again?"

Calderis's jaw tensed. "I still believe Drelian is capable of greatness, but he chose a path that betrayed the very foundation of our realm. I will not follow him into that darkness."

A long pause stretched, thick with tension.

Vaerion turned to consult with the Elders, their voices a low hum of ancient cadence. I watched them, my heart pounding, wondering if any of them had ever stood at the precipice between two worlds the way I now stood.

Finally, Vaerion turned back to us. "I have made my decision." He raised his hand, and pale blue light spilled from the crystal in his palm, washing over us like cool rain. "Lyra Wells of the Guardians. Calderis of the Enforcers. Holden Thorn of the Police."

We straightened.

"You are hereby named *The Covenant Three*—a bonded triumvirate entrusted with guarding the balance between our two realms. You will be granted full crossing rights between Elarion and the surface world, unrestricted by veil or season. You will act as protectors of the treaty, mediators of conflict, and keepers of peace."

Holden blinked. "Wait...what now?"

Vaerion didn't smile, but there was a trace of amusement in his voice. "You are part of something greater now, Chief Thorn, whether you like it or not."

Calderis lowered his head respectfully, and I mirrored the gesture, feeling the weight of the new title settle over me like a cloak. But it was Holden who broke the silence.

"Guess I'm not just the guy with the badge anymore."

Vaerion gave him a long, steady look. "You have a great deal to learn, mortal. Come. We'll begin with the boundaries of your role." He gestured for Holden to follow him.

Holden hesitated, giving me a quick glance.

"I'll be fine," I said with a small smile.

"You'd better be," he replied softly, and then followed Vaerion across the crystalline floor, leaving me alone with Calderis.

The silence that followed was not awkward—but it was charged.

Calderis studied me, his expression unreadable, his hands clasped behind his back. "You were brave," he said finally, "defying the Council."

"I'm getting used to it," I replied, then added more softly, "I couldn't let them take that from him."

"I know," he said, "and I admire that." His voice dropped slightly. "I admire a great deal about you."

That made me still.

I turned to face him fully. "Calderis..."

He took a step closer, not touching me, but near enough that I could see the tension at the corners of his mouth. "You stand in two worlds, Lyra, and you carry both burdens. Most people would collapse under the weight, but you...you thrive."

I opened my mouth to say something—anything—but the words vanished like smoke.

He looked down for a moment, then back up, his voice quieter. "There is much I cannot say. Not now. But know this—whatever comes, wherever your heart may eventually settle, I will always stand at your side. As your protector." His gaze bore into my soul. "And as your equal."

My throat felt tight. "Calderis..."

He gave me a half-smile—gentle, sad, and impossibly warm. "Go," he said, turning away before I could reply. "You should rejoin them. The mortal may need help understanding our rather...thorough contracts."

I lingered a moment longer, my heart thudding with indecision, then I turned and followed the path toward Vaerion's chambers, my mind spinning. I was Lyra Wells, Guardian of the Well, half-human, half-Dweller, and now one-third of The Covenant Three.

But mostly, I was a woman torn between two worlds...and two hearts.

Epilogue

THE SOUND of a hammer tapping gently against old wood echoed through my ancient house like a drumbeat. Holden's shoulder was doing much better after going to Michael Zaccaria's physical therapy practice. Mike and his assistant, Lauren Glaub, were Wishville's dynamic duo.

Thanks to them, my renovations were finally under way.

The house smelled faintly of paint, sawdust, and cinnamon from the maple muffins Betsy Plum had dropped off with a wink and a "just in case you need fuel for...renovating."

My front door creaked open again.

"Careful with that hinge," I called from the living room. "It's older than me and might be the only thing holding this house upright."

Holden's voice floated in, amused. "You know, for a Guardian of ancient magic, you have shockingly outdated hardware."

I poked my head out from behind the leaning bookcase I was attempting to realign. "Hey, I never said I was handy. That's *your* role in this relationship."

He gave me a crooked smile as he stepped into the room, his t-shirt dusted with sheetrock, and a toolbox slung under one muscular arm. "Is that what this is? A renovation relationship?"

"It's whatever we make it," I said.

He gave me a look at that—one of those thoughtful, too-quiet stares that made my stomach twist in a way that was entirely unfair.

The morning sun streamed through the bay window, dancing across the motes of dust floating in the air. My house was small—quirky, with slanted floors and an attic that probably housed either spiders or ancient spells—but it had always been home.

And now, with Holden kneeling beside my warped floorboards and Vex perched on the windowsill, it almost felt...full.

He reached into the floorboards, tugging loose a piece of cracked molding. "You really should have had someone do this years ago."

"I tried," I said, "but every contractor in Wishville is either booked for eternity or terrified the house is haunted since it's so old."

"Is it haunted? Like cursed?" he asked, only half-joking.

"Define curse," I said with a shrug.

He chuckled, then settled beside me with a groan. "Man, I didn't think being part of a mystical covenant would involve so much manual labor."

"Welcome to my world."

We worked in companionable silence for a while, the kind that only came from people who had been through something together—something strange and dangerous and world-altering. Between floorboard prying and loose screw collecting, I handed him a glass of iced tea, and for a moment, we just sat side by side on the dusty old rug in my living room, our legs stretched out and shoulders almost touching.

What a whirlwind it had been since we'd returned.

Rowan finally admitted he stole Samuel's research notes and gave them to me, fearing both Elarion and Dwellers, then asked Holden to pardon him. I erased him instead and set him free, none the wiser.

Poor Trip was broke and broken-hearted, the sparkle all but

gone from his wand. Evelyn skipped town after stealing all his money. Holden called a buddy of his in Boston who tracked her down and arrested her, returning the money to Trip.

Turns out she was wanted in several states.

And, finally, Weylan came clean to Calderis about having blown his cover with Samuel. Calderis let it slide, given the help he'd been, and decided to keep both Weylan and Sparks there as his eyes in the sky and ears on the ground. Sparks has proven he'd changed his ways.

I for one was happy to finally have some friends I wouldn't outlive.

"Feels good," Holden said, his voice quieter now as he broke through my thoughts. "To be useful, I mean. Not just reacting to disasters, but...building something."

"I know what you mean." I nodded. "For me, it feels good not to be alone anymore."

He looked at me, then. Really looked. And when he spoke again, it was different. "You ever think about what's next? I mean...outside of being one-third of the magical peacekeeping dream team?"

I swallowed. "Like what?"

He shrugged, but there was something fragile in the motion. "Like, where you want to be. Who you want to be with."

My heart thudded.

He didn't say more. He didn't have to. I could feel the question hanging in the air, as real and weighty as the enchanted pendant at my throat. Holden Thorn was gruff, sarcastic, maddening—and steady. Solid. New and exciting. Human in all the ways I craved when the Dweller world overwhelmed me.

But Calderis was mystery, moonlight, and duty wrapped in layers of quiet longing. We had history. He was a man from another world who saw me not as a part human girl pretending to be strong—but as someone forged from two halves, meant to walk the line between them.

I was standing in two worlds, and both were pulling me.

Holden shifted beside me. "You don't have to say anything. I just..." He rubbed the back of his neck, his eyes flicking away. "Being here, doing this—I think I just needed to know it wasn't one-sided."

I opened my mouth, but nothing came out.

Vex saved me. With a sharp meow, he leaped from the windowsill and padded across the room, his head tilted as if he'd just heard something none of us could.

"Vex?" I asked, rising.

He darted to the bookcase we'd been adjusting earlier and pawed at the floorboard just behind it. Not the one we had repaired but another, a thinner plank, warped along one edge.

Holden was already moving, pulling tools from his belt. "Looks loose."

I crouched beside him, my heart suddenly racing. "Careful," I whispered.

With one quick motion, he pried the board up and revealed a narrow hollow space beneath it. Nestled inside, surrounded by dust and forgotten fragments of dried lavender, was a delicate silver box no bigger than my palm.

My breath caught.

I reached out, my fingers trembling, and lifted it carefully from its hiding place. The lid bore a carved symbol—three spirals interlocked like a triad.

"I've seen this before," I murmured. "My mother wore a pendant just like this."

Holden leaned closer. "What is it?"

I flipped the latch and slowly opened the box. Inside was a folded piece of parchment, brittle with age but still legible. The script was curved and elegant, unmistakably Dweller. My mother's handwriting.

> *Lyra,*
> *If you're reading this, it means the well still speaks, and I have not yet returned. Know that I never left you by choice. There are*

things I had to protect—truths buried beneath Elarion, secrets not even Vaerion knows. If you seek answers, find the key within the Whisper Woods. Trust the spiral path. It will take you to the truth— and maybe, to me.

—Serenna

I pressed a hand to my mouth.

Holden put a steadying hand on my back. "She's alive?"

"I don't know," I whispered, "but she left this for me. She wanted me to find her."

He stared at the letter, then back at me. "Then we'll find her."

Something about the way he said *we* made my heart flutter and ache all at once.

I didn't know what path lay ahead. I didn't know if I'd find my mother, or what truth she'd risked everything to hide, but I knew I wouldn't face it alone.

Not anymore.

And as I looked around my tiny, crooked house—at the strong human man rebuilding my floors and the magical cat prowling my shadows and the magnificent Dweller watching out for me from another realm—I realized that maybe just maybe I didn't have to choose between worlds just yet.

Maybe I could belong to both.

Maybe I already did.

Dweller Powers Linked to Water, Lava, and the Core

Because Dwellers live beneath the well and near the Earth's hidden layers, their powers tie into subterranean elements—water tables, magma flows, and the planet's inner energy.

1. Water Affinity

1. **Aquifer Calling** – ability to summon fresh water from underground springs.
2. **Mists and Veils** – conjuring fog or vapor to obscure vision.
3. **Current Shaping** – manipulating underground rivers and directing them to flood or recede.
4. **Memory Pools** – reflections in water that reveal truths, memories, or wishes.

2. Lava and Magma Affinity

1. **Ember Pulse** – channeling molten heat into bursts of energy or fiery weaponry.
2. **Obsidian Crafting** – forming weapons, keys, or charms instantly from cooled lava.
3. **Seismic Heat** – creating pockets of intense heat to deter intruders or destroy evidence.
4. **Infernal Glow** – eyes or markings flare with inner magma-light when power is used.

3. Core/Earth Affinity

1. **Seismic Whisper** – sensing tremors or distant footsteps through the ground.
2. **Stone Weaving** – reshaping rock, tunnels, or caverns for defense or concealment.

3. **Core Binding** – drawing strength from geothermal energy, boosting speed or stamina.
4. **Gravity Veil** – slightly altering pull of gravity around them (leaping, pulling objects down).

4. Hybrid Powers (Water + Fire/Core)

1. **Steam Veil** – merging water and magma to create blinding, scalding mist.
2. **Healing Springs** – heated water with mineral-rich, magical properties for mending wounds.
3. **Crystalline Growth** – forming luminous crystal clusters where water meets lava under pressure.
4. **Pressure Command** – controlling deep-earth pressure, causing geysers or controlled quakes.

Lyra's Hybrid Powers

As the only half-human, half-Dweller, Lyra bridges above-ground elements (air, light, celestial forces) with subterranean ones (water, magma, core). Her uniqueness gives her powers that no full Dweller can access.

1. Celestial Affinity

1. **Sunfire Touch** – channeling warmth and light to heal or inspire courage.
2. **Moonveil** – manipulating moonlight for illusions, cloaking, or calming emotions.
3. **Star Echo** – heightened intuition or visions tied to constellations and night sky patterns.
4. **Skycall** – Influence over breezes, gusts, or even guiding birds.

2. Core Affinity

1. **Seismic Sense** – feeling vibrations through earth, sensing danger or hidden chambers.
2. **Lumen Wells** – pulling luminous energy from underground crystals.
3. **Magma Ward** – summoning protective heat barriers or obsidian shards.
4. **Aqua Vein** – drawing water from beneath the ground in times of need.

3. Hybrid/Balance Powers

1. **Eclipse State** – when sun and moon energies align, she can blend surface light with core fire for immense bursts of power.
2. **Breath of Worlds** – exhaling mist that merges steam, air, and memory-infused water.
3. **Harmony Pulse** – ability to temporarily stabilize cracks between worlds.
4. **Dual Sight** – seeing both surface illusions and subterranean truths simultaneously.

Vex (half-cat, half-Whispen)

Whisper Magic
Abilities:

1. **Shadow Phase** – slip between shadows in both realms.
2. **Mist Purr** – calming veil of vapor.
3. **Mind Whisper** – can communicate with others through their mind

Books By Kari Lee Townsend

A WISHVILLE MYSTERY

The Well-Kept Secret

The Well-Laid Trap

The Well-Hidden Clue

The Well-Placed Lie

KALLI BALLAS MYSTERY

Mind Over Murder

Two Cents of Doom

A Touch of Malice

An Inkling of Evil

Mayhem on the Mind

Trouble for Your Thoughts

CECE MONROE MYSTERY

Harmful Habits

SUNNY MEADOWS MYSTERY

Tempest in the Tea Leaves

Corpse in the Crystal Ball

Trouble in the Tarot

Shenanigans in the Shadows

Perish in the Palm

Hazard in the Horoscope

Chaos and Cold Feet

Murder in the Meditation

<u>SUNNY MEADOWS & KALLIE BALLAS CROSSOVER</u>

Cruising into Danger

Road Trip to Ruin

Bachelors, Badeges & Bad Luck

My Big Fat Fatal Wedding

<u>DIGITAL DIVA</u>

Talk to the Hand

Rise of the Phenoteens

Books By Kari Lee Harmon

COLDWATER COVE

Dark Seas

Frozen Waters

Dangerous Thaw

Deadly Frost

STANDALONE NOVELS

Valley of Secrets

Until Tomorrow

Project Produce

Love Lessons

LAKEHOUSE TREASURES NOVELLAS

James

Amber

Meghan

Brook

MERRY SCROOG-MAS NOVELLAS

Naughty or Nice

Sleigh Bells Ring

Jingle all the Way

TRIPLE R RANCH

Destiny Wears Spurs

Spurred by Fate

PORTRAIT OF A WOMAN

Resilient

Resourceful

Rebellious

Reclusive

National Bestselling Author, Agatha, RT Reviewer's Choice & Golden Duck Award Nominee. Kari lives in Central New York with her husband & Samoyeds. She's a lover of wine & travel (especially cruising), obsessed with reality TV, and loves a good book with at least some mystery, romance & humor. She writes cozy mysteries & upper middle grade as Kari Lee Townsend, as well as suspense, romance, romantic comedy & women's fiction as Kari Lee Harmon. To keep up with all of Kari Lee's books, check out her website, join her newsletter, and follow her on Amazon, Goodreads, and Bookbub! All links are on her website.

https://www.karileetownsend.com